No Way

NO WAY

Natalia Ginzburg

Translated by
Sheila Cudahy

A Helen and Kurt Wolff Book
Harcourt Brace Jovanovich
New York and London

Printed in the United States of America

Library of Congress Cataloging in Publication Data
Ginzburg, Natalia.
No way.
"A Helen and Kurt Wolff book."
Translation of Caro Michele.
I.   Title.
PZ3.G437No   [PQ4817.I5]   853'.9'12   74–7069
ISBN 0–15–167674–7

First edition

B C D E

No Way

1

A woman named Adriana got out of bed in her new house. It was snowing. That day was her birthday. She was forty-three. The house was out in the country. She could see the town on a little hill in the distance. It was one and a quarter miles away. The city was more than nine miles away. She had lived in the house for ten days. She put on a bathrobe of tobacco-colored voile and slipped her long thin feet into old brown slippers edged with dirty white fur. She went down into the kitchen and made a cup of instant coffee into which she crumbled crackers. On the table lay some apple cores, which she wrapped in old newspaper to save for the rabbits. She did not actually own rabbits as yet but made plans nevertheless because the milkman had promised to get them for her. She went into the living room and opened the blinds. The mirror behind the sofa caught her tall figure, the short wavy copper-colored hair, small head, long neck, and wide, sad green eyes. She greeted and contemplated her image. Then she sat down at the desk and wrote a letter to her only son.

Dear Michael,

I am writing primarily to tell you that your father is ill. Go and see him. He says he hasn't seen you for days. I went yesterday. It was the first Thursday of the month. While I was waiting for him at Canova, his servant telephoned to say he was sick. So I went up to the house. He was in bed. I thought he looked worn out. He has bags under his eyes and his color is poor. He has pains in his stomach. He eats nothing and, of course, goes on smoking.

When you go to see him, don't take your usual twenty-five pairs of dirty socks. That servant whose name is Henry or Frederick, I don't recall which, can't cope with your dirty laundry right now. He is overworked and exhausted. He can't sleep at night because your father keeps calling him. Furthermore, this is his first job as a domestic. He worked in an electrical repair shop before. What's more, he is utterly stupid.

If you have a lot of dirty laundry, bring it here to me. I have a woman named Cloti. She came five days ago. She is not very pleasant. But since she always sulks and the chances of her staying on the job are slim, I don't care if you arrive with a suitcase full of stuff that needs to be washed and ironed. You may bring it here. However, I remind you that there are plenty of good laundries near your basement apartment. You are old enough to look after yourself. You will be twenty-two soon. By the way, today is my birthday. The twins gave me a pair of bedroom slippers. However, I like my old ones. And I also want to say that it would be a good thing if you would wash your handkerchiefs and socks every night instead of letting them pile up under your bed for weeks, but I have never been able to get you to understand this.

I waited for the doctor, one Povo or Covo; I didn't get the name. He lives on the floor above. I could not figure out what he thinks about your father's illness. He says it is an ulcer, which we knew. He says your father ought to go to the hospital, but your father won't hear of it.

Maybe you think I ought to move in with your father and take care of him. I considered it for a moment but I don't think I'll do it. I am afraid of sickness. I am afraid of other people's sickness, not of my own, but then I have never had a serious illness. When my father had diverticulitis, I took a trip to Holland. I knew perfectly well it was not diverticulitis. It was cancer. So when he died, I was away. I regret it. Still the truth is that at a certain point in our lives we crumble our regrets like biscuits in our morning coffee.

Then, too, I don't know how your father would react if I should arrive tomorrow with my suitcase. He has been self-conscious with me for many years. And I became self-conscious with him. There is nothing worse than self-consciousness between two people who have loathed each other. They have nothing more to say to each other. They are mutually thankful to be past the point of hitting and scratching, but this sort of gratitude finds no outlet in words. After the separation, your father and I acquired the polite and tiresome habit of meeting for tea at Canova on the first Thursday of every month. It was not his idea or mine. His cousin Lillino, the one who is the lawyer in Mantua, had advised us to meet regularly and your father always listens to him. According to his cousin, we were supposed to keep in touch and to get together once in a while to discuss matters of mutual interest. However, those hours spent at Canova were torture for your father and me. Since your father is methodical in his disorderly way, he decided we ought to sit at that little table from five o'clock to seven-thirty. Every so often he would sigh and look at the clock, and I found this humiliating. He would tilt back in his chair and scratch his large black unkempt head of hair. He seemed to me a weary old panther. We talked about you children. However, he could not care less about your sisters. You are the only one who counts. From the very beginning he decided that you are the only thing in the world worthy of tenderness and veneration. We talked about you. He stated instantly that I had never understood a thing about you and that he alone really knew you. So that took care of that subject. We were so afraid of contradicting one another that every topic seemed dangerous and we would drop it. You children knew that we met on those afternoons but what you didn't know was that it was his damned cousin who advised us to meet. I see that I have used the past tense here. I really think your father is very unwell and that we will never meet again at Canova every first Thursday of the month.

If you were not such a scatterbrain I would tell you to leave your basement apartment and move back to Via San Sebastianello. You could get up during the night instead of the servant. After all, you don't have anything in particular to do. Viola has her house to look after and Angelica has her job and her little girl. The twins are in school and anyway they are young. Besides, your father can't bear the twins. He doesn't get along very well with Viola or Angelica. As to his own sisters, Cecilia is old and he and Matilde detest one another. Matilde is staying with me now and will remain through the winter. In any case, the only person in the world your father loves and tolerates near him is you. However, given your life style, I realize it is better that you stay on in your apartment. If you were at your father's, you would add to the disorder and drive that servant up the wall.

Here is something else I want to tell you. I have received a letter from a person who says her name is Mara Castorelli and that she met me last year at a party in your apartment. I recall the party but there were so many people that I don't remember anyone clearly. The letter was forwarded to me from my old address in Via dei Villini. This person asks if I would help her find a job. She writes from a boardinghouse where she cannot remain because it is too expensive for her. She says she has had a baby and she wants to come here to show me this pretty baby. I have not answered her yet. I used to like babies but now I haven't the slightest desire to coo over a baby. I am too tired. I would like to know from you who this person is and what sort of work she wants, because she doesn't explain it clearly. At first I didn't take this letter very seriously, but then at a certain point I wondered if the baby could be yours. What I can't understand is how this person came to write to me. Her handwriting is weird. I asked your father if he knew a cerain Martorelli, a girl friend of yours. He said he didn't and then began to talk about the Pastorella cheese that he used to take with him when he went sailing, but, of course, it is impossible to have a sensible conversation with your father. However, little by little, the idea that this baby is yours stuck in my mind. Last night after supper I got my car out again. That always takes a great effort. I went into town to telephone you but you are never there. On my return, I got to crying. In part, I was thinking of your father who is in such bad shape and in part, I was thinking of you. If by any chance the baby of this Martorello is yours, what will you do since you don't know how to do anything. You didn't want to finish school. I don't find your paintings of houses collapsing and owls in flight very beautiful. Your father says they are beautiful and that I do not understand painting. It seems to me that they resemble the paintings your father did when he was young, only worse. I can't figure it out. I wish you would let me know what to reply to this Martorelli and if I should send her money. She doesn't ask, but clearly she wants some.

I am still without a telephone. I have been to hurry them up I don't know how many times, but no one has come. Please, you go to the telephone company. It is not much to ask of you because the office is not far from you. Perhaps that friend of yours, Oswald, who gave you the apartment, knows somebody at the telephone company. The twins say that Oswald has a cousin there. Find out if this is so. It was nice of him to give you the apartment rent free, but a basement is a dark place in which to paint. Maybe that is why you do all those owls, because you are painting down there with the lights on and you think it is night outside. It must also be damp and it's a good thing I gave you that German stove for heating.

I don't suppose you will come to wish me a "happy birthday," because I don't believe you remember it. Neither Viola nor Angelica will come. I know because I spoke to both of them yesterday on the telephone and found they could not. I like this house but I do find it inconvenient to be so far from everyone. I thought the air here would be good for the twins, but they disappear for the whole day. They go to school on their motorbikes and eat at a pizza place in the center of town. They do their homework at a friend's house and come home when it is dark. I worry until they get back, because I don't like them to be on the road when it is already dark. Three days ago your Aunt Matilde arrived. She would like to go and see your father, but he has said he doesn't want to see her. They have been on bad terms for years. I wrote Matilde to come because she was depressed and nervous and short of money. She has made a bad investment in certain Swiss funds. I asked her to help the twins with their lessons, but the twins make themselves scarce. I will have to put up with her but don't know how I will manage that.

Maybe I made a mistake in buying this house. The milkman is going to get me some rabbits. When he does, I wish you would come and build the hutch. For the moment I plan to keep them in the woodshed. The twins would like a horse.

I must tell you that the real reason was that I did not want to be running into Philip all the time. He lives so near Via dei Villini, and I was always running into him. It was painful to meet him. He is well. His wife is having a baby in the spring. My God, how is it that all these babies are always born when people are fed up and can no longer put up with them. One has seen too many of these children.

Now I must stop writing and give this letter to Matilde who is going to do the shopping and I shall stay to watch the snow and to read the *Pensées* of Pascal.

Mother

After she had finished and sealed the letter she went back down to the kitchen. She greeted and kissed the twins Bebetta and Nanetta, aged fourteen. They had identical blond ponytails, wore identical navy-blue blazers, identical plaid knee socks and went to school on identical motorbikes. She greeted and kissed her sister-in-law Matilde, a fat old maid with a mannish haircut. A shock of her straight white hair was always falling into her eyes, and she would toss it back with a bold gesture. There was no sign of Cloti, the maid, in the kitchen. Matilde wanted to call her. She remarked that the maid got up a quarter of an hour later each morning and each morning complained bitterly that her mattress was lumpy. Finally Cloti did appear and slid along the hall dressed in a very short sky-blue bathrobe and with her long gray hair loose about her shoulders. After a moment she came out of the bathroom wearing a stiff new brown apron. She had put her hair up with two combs. She began to make the beds and pulled at the covers in a sad lethargic manner, expressing with every gesture her desire to quit. Matilde put on a Tirolean cape and announced she would go on foot to do the marketing, praising the snow and healthy freezing air in her deep strong voice. She ordered the maid to cook the onions she had seen hanging in the kitchen. Cloti replied in a dull monotone that those onions were all rotted.

By now Adriana had dressed. She wore tobacco-colored stockings and a sand-colored pullover. She sat by the fire in the living room but she did not read the *Pensées* of Pascal. She read nothing and did not even look out at the snow, because all of a sudden she felt a loathing for that snow-clotted landscape outside her window. Instead, she rested her head in one hand and with the other caressed her feet and ankles in the tobacco-colored stockings, and so she spent the morning.

2

A man named Oswald Ventura went into a boardinghouse on Annibaliano Square. He was a sturdy, well-built man and wore a raincoat. He had fair hair turning gray, a florid complexion, and hazel eyes. There was always an uncertain smile on his lips.

A girl he knew had telephoned him to come and get her. She wanted to move out of her boardinghouse. Someone had lent her an apartment in Via dei Prefetti.

The girl was sitting in the lobby, dressed in a turquoise-blue knitted blouse, dark purple pants, and a black coat embroidered with silver dragons. On the floor at her feet were bags and sacks and a baby in a yellow plastic carrier.

"I have been sitting here like a fool, waiting for you for an hour," she said.

Oswald gathered up all the bags and sacks and carried them to the door.

"See that girl with the curly hair by the elevator? She had the room next to mine. She was very nice to me. I owe her a lot, including money. Give her a smile."

Oswald offered his uncertain smile to the curly-haired girl.

"My brother has come to get me. I am going home. To-morrow I will bring back the thermos and everything," Mara said. She and the curly-haired girl kissed each other on the cheek.

Oswald picked up the suitcase, the bags, and sacks again, and they went out.

"How come I am your brother?" he asked.

"She was very nice, so I told her you were my brother. Nice people enjoy meeting one's relatives."

"Do you owe her a lot of money?"

"Very little. Do you want to pay her back?"

"No," Oswald said.

"I told her I would bring it tomorrow, but I won't. They will never see me in that place again. Some day I'll send it to her."

"When?"

"When I have a job."

"And the thermos?"

"Perhaps I won't return the thermos either. Anyway, she has another one."

Oswald's car was parked on the other side of the square. It was snowing and windy. Mara walked along tilting her head under a wide-brimmed hat of black felt. She was a pale, dark-haired girl, very small and very thin with wide hips. Her coat with the dragons flapped in the wind and her sandals sank in the snow.

"Didn't you have anything warmer to wear?" he said.

"No. All my stuff is in a trunk at the place of two of my friends. On the Via Cassia."

"Elisabeth is in the car," he said.

"Elisabeth? Who is she?"

"My daughter."

Elisabeth sat curled up on the back seat. She was nine years old. Her hair was carrot colored and she wore a sweater and a checked blouse. In her arms she held a dog with a tawny coat and long ears. The yellow plastic carrier was put next to her.

"How come you dragged along the little girl with that beast?" Mara said.

"Elisabeth was at her grandmother's, and I went to fetch her," he said.

"You always have chores. You always do things that other people want. When will you have your own life?"

"What makes you think I don't have a life of my own?" he said.

"Hold onto that dog so it doesn't lick my baby, Elisabeth," she said.

"Exactly how old is the baby?" Oswald asked.

"Twenty-two days. Don't you remember that he is twenty-two days old? I left the hospital two weeks ago. The chief floor nurse recommended that boardinghouse to me. But I couldn't stay there. It was dirty. I hated to put my feet on the bath mat. It was a green rubber mat. You know how disgusting those green rubber mats in boardinghouses can be."

"Yes, I know."

"Besides I was spending a lot. And they were rude. I need kindness. I always needed it, but since I have had the baby I need it even more."

"I understand."

"Don't you need kindness?"

"Tremendously."

"They said I rang the bell too often. I rang because I needed a lot of things. Boiled water. Then other things. The baby gets a mixed feeding. It is very complicated. You have to weigh the baby, then nurse him, then weigh him again and give him the other milk. I would ring the bell ten times. They never came. Finally they would bring the boiled water, but I always doubted whether they really had boiled it."

"You could have boiled it in your room."

"No. It wasn't allowed. And they always forgot something. The fork."

"The fork?"

"To beat the powdered milk. I had told them to bring me a saucepan, a cup, a fork, and a spoon each time. All in a napkin. The fork was always missing. I would ask for a fork, but one that had been boiled, and they would be rude. Sometimes I thought I ought to tell them to boil the napkin, too. But I was afraid that would enrage them."

"I certainly think it would have enraged them."

"To weigh the baby I went to the room of that girl with the curly hair whom you saw. She has a baby, too, and she had a scale for nursing babies. However, she told me very politely that I was not to appear in her room at two in the morning. So at night I had to guess at it. Maybe your wife has one of those scales at home."

"Is there a scale for infants at home, Elisabeth?" Oswald asked.

"I don't know. I don't think so."

"Almost everyone has one of those scales in the cellar," said Mara.

"I don't think we do," Elisabeth said.

"But I need a scale."

"You can rent one from the drugstore," said Oswald.

"How can I rent one when I haven't a cent?"

"What sort of work are you thinking of looking for?" he asked.

"I don't know. Maybe I can sell secondhand books in your shop."

"No. That's not possible."

"Why?"

"It's a hole in the wall. There is no space to move around. And I already have someone who helps me."

"I saw her. A sort of cow."

"That is Mrs. Schlitz. She was a governess in Ada's family. Ada, my wife."

"Call me Schlitz. I'll be your beer. No, I will be your cow."

They were in Trastevere in a little square with a fountain. Elisabeth got out with the dog.

"So long, Elisabeth," Oswald said.

Elisabeth slipped into the doorway of a small red building. She disappeared.

"She said almost nothing," said Mara.

"She is shy."

"Shy and rude. She didn't even look at the baby. As if there was nothing there. I don't like the color of your house."

"It is not my house. My wife lives there with Elisabeth. I live alone."

"I know. I had forgotten. You are always talking about your wife, so I never remember that you live alone. Give me your phone number; I have only that of the shop. It could be useful to have it at night."

"I beg you not to call me at night. I am a light sleeper."

"You have never asked me to your place. This past summer when we met on the street and I had that big belly and told you I wanted to take a shower, you said there wasn't any water in your neighborhood."

"It was true."

"I was staying with nuns and one could take a shower only on Sunday."

"How did you end up with nuns?"

"Because I paid very little. Before that I was living on Via Cassia. Then I fought with those friends of mine. They got angry because I broke a movie camera. They told me to go back to my cousins in Novi Ligure. They gave me the money for the trip. They weren't mean. But what would I do in Novi Ligure? I had been out of touch with my cousins for some time. Then if they saw me arrive with that belly, they would have dropped dead. And there's lots of them in the family and they have no money. But he is better than she is."

"He who?"

"He. The one who lives on Via Cassia. His wife is tight-fisted when it comes to money. He is nicer. He works in television. He told me that as soon as I had had the baby he would give me a job. Maybe I'll telephone him."

"Why maybe?"

"Because he asked me if I knew English and I said yes, but that isn't true. I don't know a word of English."

The apartment in Via dei Prefetti was a railroad flat of three rooms. In the back room there was a glass door with a ragged awning. The door opened onto a balcony facing a courtyard. On the balcony stood a laundry rack on which hung a nightgown of pale mauve flannel.

"The laundry rack will be useful," Mara said.

"Whose nightgown is that?" asked Oswald.

"Not mine. I have never been here before. The apartment belongs to a girl I know. She doesn't need it. I don't know whose nightgown that is. In fact, she doesn't even sleep in a nightgown. She sleeps in the nude. She read somewhere that the Finns sleep in the nude and get very strong."

"You took this apartment without seeing it?"

"Of course. I am not paying for it. They are lending it to me. This dear friend of mine is lending it to me."

The back room contained a round table covered with red-and-white checked oilcloth and a double bed with a pale mauve chenille spread. In the middle room there was a small stove, a wash basin, a broom, a calendar on the wall, and plates and pots on the floor. There was nothing in the front room.

"You boil the water," she said. "Everything is here. They told me everything I need is here. A bowl, cup, fork, and spoon."

"I don't see any forks," Oswald said.

"Christ. I have no luck with forks. I'll use a spoon."

"I don't see any spoons, either. Only knives."

"Christ. Well, I have a plastic spoon. Curly Hair gave it to me. The only trouble is one can't boil it. It melts. That's the trouble with plastic."

She lifted the baby from the carrier and put him on the bed. The baby had long black hair. He was wrapped in a flowered towel. He stretched. Two feet in enormous blue booties emerged from the towel.

"You have no luck with chairs, either," Oswald said. He went out on the balcony and picked up a canvas chair with a torn seat. He brought it inside and sat down.

"I'm unlucky in everything," she said. Seated on the bed, she opened her blouse and nursed the baby.

"What about weighing him? You didn't weigh the baby," he said.

"How can I weigh him without a scale? I'll have to guess at it."

"Do you want me to go to the drugstore and rent you a scale?"

"Are you willing to pay for it?"

"Yes, I'm willing."

"I thought you were stingy. You always said you were stingy and poor. You always said you don't have a cent and that even the bed you sleep on belongs to your wife."

"In fact I am stingy and poor but I'm willing to rent the scale."

"Later. Go later. Now just sit in the chair. I like to have someone around when I am mixing the powdered milk. I am afraid of making a mistake, of getting lumps in the milk. At the boardinghouse I counted on Curly Hair. I would call her and she came right away. Not at night, though. She didn't come then."

"I can't stay here forever," he said. "Later I have to go to see my wife."

"You are separated. What do you have to see her for?"

"I go to visit my little girl and to visit her, too. I visit them almost every day."

"Why are you separated?"

"We were too different to live together."

"How different?"

"Different. She rich, I poor. She very active, I lazy. She has an obsession for interior decoration."

"And you have no obsession for interior decoration?"

"None."

"When you married her, did you hope to become richer and less lazy?"

"Yes. Or maybe I hoped she would become lazier and poorer."

"Instead nothing happened."

"Nothing. She made a certain effort to become lazier, but she suffered. While she was lying down, she kept on dreaming up projects. I felt as if I was next to a boiling cauldron."

"What were the projects?"

"Oh, she always has projects. Houses to be remodeled. Old aunts to get settled. Furniture to be refinished. Garages to be turned into galleries. Bitches to breed to dogs. Slip covers to be dyed."

"And what efforts did you make to become less lazy and richer?"

"At the beginning I made a slight effort to become a little bit richer. However, they were very slight and very clumsy attempts. Anyway, she didn't care that much about my earning money. She wanted me to write books. She really wanted that. She said it. She expected it. That was terribly hard on me."

"All you needed to do was to tell her you didn't have any books to write."

"I wasn't so sure. Sometimes I think that I would have written them if she had not expected it. But I was always surrounded by her stubborn, benevolent, vast, encumbering expectation. I felt it even in my sleep. It was killing me."

"So you left."

"It all happened with incredible calm. One day I simply told her that I wanted to live by myself again. She didn't seem shocked. For some time her expectation had diminished. She seemed more or less her normal self but now she had two little lines at the corners of her mouth."

"And the shop? Does the shop also belong to your wife?"

"No, it belongs to my uncle who lives in Varese, but I have been in it so many years that it seems mine."

"Yet when you went to live by yourself, you didn't write books. Obviously you only know how to sell books, other people's books."

"True. Even then I didn't write books. How did you know?"

"Michael told me. He said you are lazy and write nothing."

"It's true."

"I would like it if your wife came here and decorated this apartment for me."

"My wife?"

"Yes, your wife. If she remodels garages, she can do this place over."

"My wife? My wife would come immediately. She would call in plasterers, electricians. She would also change your life. She would put the baby in a day-care center. She would send you to learn English. She would not give you a moment's peace. She would throw away the clothes you are wearing. The coat with the dragons would be thrown in the trash."

"But it's so great."

"It is not her sort of thing, the coat with the dragons. No, it's not Ada's sort of thing."

"Curly Hair said that maybe I can stay with them in

19

Sicily. Her husband is in Trapani opening a snack bar. If it works out well, they would give me a job. They need someone to do the bookkeeping."

"Do you know how to keep accounts?"

"Almost anybody can keep accounts."

"But maybe not you."

"Well, Curly Hair thinks I can. They would give me a room in their apartment over the snack bar. Besides doing the books, I would have to take care of the house and look after their baby along with mine. Sometimes people make millions with these snack bars."

"Have you ever been to Trapani?"

"Never. Curly Hair is sort of scared. She is not sure how she will like Trapani. And then she isn't certain how this snack bar thing will work out. Her husband has gone broke twice with restaurants. The money is hers. Then, too, she went to a fortuneteller with her husband. The fortuneteller told them to stay away from cities in the South."

"And then?"

"Then nothing. She got heart fibrillations. She said it would be a great comfort to have me nearby. If I don't know what to do, I'll go."

"I don't advise you to go."

"Do you advise me to do something else?"

"I don't advise anything. I never give advice to anyone."

"Will you see Michael tonight?"

"I don't know. You are not expecting advice from Michael?"

"No. Still, it would be nice if he came here. I haven't seen him for ages. I went to see him in his basement. I still had my big belly. I told him I wanted to take a shower, but he said there wasn't any hot water. According to him, cold water would be bad for me."

"You have no luck with showers, either."

"I don't know what I am not unlucky with. When the

baby was born, I telephoned him. He said he was coming but he didn't. I wrote his mother a few days ago."

"You wrote to his mother? What possessed you?"

"Oh, just like that. I know her. I saw her once. In the letter I gave the address of the boardinghouse. I was thinking of staying there; then I changed my mind. I told Curly Hair that if any letters came for me to forward them to your shop. I didn't want to give this address to Curly Hair. She might drop in. I told Curly Hair a few lies. I told her I was going to a delightful apartment with wall-to-wall carpeting in some rooms and rugs in others. I told her I was going to stay with my brother who is an antiquarian. I made you into an antiquarian. Instead, you are just a secondhand book seller."

"Above all, you made me be your brother."

"Yes. Really I have a brother, but he is little. Eleven years old. His name is Paul. He lives with those cousins. I named the baby Paul Michael. You know I could take Michael to court, because I am a minor. If I took him to court, he would have to marry me."

"Do you want to marry Michael?"

"No. It would be like marrying my little brother."

"Then why do you want to take him to court?"

"I don't want to take him to court. I haven't the slightest intention of taking him to court. I am only saying that if I want to, I can. Go and see if that pot is boiling."

"It's been boiling for some time," he said.

"Then turn it off."

"You aren't a minor," he said. "You are twenty-two years old. I saw your identity card."

"Yes, that's true. I was twenty-two in March. But how come you saw my identity card?"

"You gave it to me. You wanted to show me how bad the photograph was."

"True. Now I remember. I often tell lies."

"It seems to me you tell useless lies."

"Not always useless. Sometimes there is a point to them. When I told Curly Hair about the carpeting, it was because I wanted her to envy me. I was fed up with her feeling sorry for me. You get fed up with people always feeling sorry for you. And sometimes you are so down that the only way to feel better is to invent stories."

"You told me that you don't know whether or not this baby is Michael's."

"I really don't know. I am not one hundred per cent sure. I think it is his. However, at that time, I was sleeping with a lot of guys. I don't know what got into me. Then when I discovered I was pregnant, I thought I wanted the baby. I was positive I wanted it. I had never been as sure of anything. I wrote my sister in Genoa and she sent me money for an abortion. I wrote back that I was keeping the money but no abortion. She replied that I was crazy."

"Can't you get your sister to come here? Haven't you anyone you could ask to come?"

"No. My sister is now married to a farm surveyor. I wrote her when the baby was born. He answered, this appraiser whom I had never even seen. He wrote me that they were moving to Germany. He wrote me to go to hell. Not in so many words, but almost."

"I see."

"When a woman has a baby, she wants to show it to everybody. That is why I would like Michael to see it. We are great friends. We spent such great days together. Sometimes he is such fun. I went around with others, but with him I had fun. Don't think I want to marry him. It never entered my mind. I am not in love with him at all. I have been in love only once. It was in Novi Ligure. He was my cousin's husband. I never made love to him. My cousin was always there."

"Michael says he will get you some money. He will ask his family. He will come. Sometime or other he'll come. But he says newborn babies scare him."

"I want the money. I know he asked you to be nice to me. You would have been nice anyway, even if he hadn't asked you. You are naturally kind. It's strange I have never made love with you. It never entered my mind, or yours either, I guess. I wonder if you aren't queer. But I guess not."

"I'm not," he said.

"But it never entered your head to make love with me?"

"Never entered my head."

"You think me ugly?"

"No."

"Pretty?"

"Yes. Pretty."

"But I don't appeal to you? I leave you cold?"

"To tell the truth, yes."

"Go to hell," she said. "That is not a nice thing to have said to one's face."

"The baby is sleeping. He is not eating any more."

"Right. He is scary, this baby."

"He is not at all scary. He does nothing but sleep."

"Even when he is sleeping, he is scary. I know I'm in a mess. Don't think I don't know."

"What is the matter with you? Why are you crying now?"

"Go and beat the milk."

"I have never beaten milk in my life," Oswald said.

"It doesn't matter. Read the instructions on the box. For Christ's sake, help me."

3

December 2, 1970

Dear Michael,

Last night Oswald came and told me that you have left for London. I am stunned and confused. Oswald said that you looked in on your father for a moment, but he was sleeping. You looked in. What good is that? Perhaps you were not aware that your father is very sick. That Povo or Covo said that he has to go into the hospital today.

You needed shirts and woolen things. Oswald says you are thinking of staying there for the entire winter. You could have telephoned me. You might have called me at the public phone in town as you have done other times. If they don't install the phone here I will go crazy. I would have come to the airport and I would have brought you some clothes. Oswald says you left with your cotton twill trousers and red knitted shirt and nothing or almost nothing else. Oswald says all your laundry, both clean and dirty, is still in your apartment. He didn't remember whether or not you had your loden coat with you. Then he remembered that you had it. This comforted me a little.

He says you arrived at his place early in the morning. According to him the idea of leaving for London and attending an art school to study sculpture was something you have been thinking about for some time. Apparently you have been fed up with all those owls for some time. I understand that. I am writing to this address, which Oswald gave me but he says it is temporary. The fact that Oswald vaguely knows the elderly lady who is renting you a room reassures me a little, but very little. Don't think that I do not realize that your departure was a flight. I am not a fool. I ask you to write me immediately and explain clearly from what or from whom you wanted to run. Oswald was not clear about it. Either he didn't want to tell me or he didn't know.

Anyway, you have gone. I returned to Oswald the three hundred thousand lire he had lent you. That is, I repaid them by check to his wife. Oswald says his wife always has cash in the house. If that had not been the case you would not have been able to leave since it was Saturday. Oswald came to my place at ten o'clock last night. He was dead tired from having struggled at police headquarters to get your passport, which had expired, and from having driven you to the airport and then having to go outside Rome to get back some car or other belonging to his wife that you had lent to God only knows whom. He had not eaten and I had nothing in the house except various kinds of cheese that Matilde had bought at the supermarket in the morning. I put all these cheeses before him and he gobbled them up. Matilde entertained him on the subject of the French Impressionists. Matilde tossed her lock of hair and smoked with her cigarette holder and walked up and down with her hand in the pockets of her cardigan. I could have killed her. I wanted her to leave so that I could question Oswald about you. The twins were there also playing Ping-pong. Finally everyone went to bed.

I asked him if you had left because of that Mara Castorelli who wrote to me and who has a baby. Oswald told me that the baby is not yours. According to him the girl has nothing to do with your departure. He says she is only a poor and stupid girl without money, without a blanket and without a chair, and he is thinking of taking her the blankets and chairs from your apartment where they are of no use to anyone now. He asked me if he could bring her that green stove with the decorations, the German stove, that is. I said it would be necessary to remove the pipe from the wall and that might be complicated. I remember the day when I went to buy that stove for you, and therefore it was dear to me. Undoubtedly you will consider it stupid to be fond of a stove. Oswald told me you never lit it because you never remembered to order wood and that you used an electric heater instead. Finally I said he could do whatever he wanted with the chairs and the stove. I asked him if by chance you might have got mixed up with some dangerous political splinter groups. I always have a terrible fear that you could end up with the Tupamaros. He said he didn't know what sort of people you were going around with recently. He said it was quite possible that you were afraid of something. He wasn't clear.

I can't decide if I like him. He is kind. He is so very kind that one ends up feeling too full, as if one had eaten too much candy. He has that florid face that is always smiling. But I can't find anything to smile about. For a moment, looking at him, I wondered if he were a homosexual. I have never understood how you got to be friends, you a boy and he a man of thirty-six or thirty-eight. You will say that there's no end to my worries about you.

He doesn't have a cousin at the telephone company, but he thinks that Ada, his wife, may have an acquaintance there. He promised to ask her. I don't know what we would do without this Ada. She gave you the money so you could leave. She telephoned someone about your passport, otherwise I don't know how you would have got your passport. You ought to write and thank her. Oswald says she was up at seven in the morning when he went there. She was cleaning the brick floor with kerosene. I have brick floors here, too, but we have never cleaned them with kerosene. In fact, they do look dull. I guess Cloti doesn't clean them with anything.

The morning before last Matilde came along with me to visit your father. When we got there, he was sitting on the bed, smoking and telephoning so he didn't give her the impression of being very sick. He was talking on the telephone with that architect. I don't know if you know that the week before your father got sick, he bought a tower on the Isola del Giglio. He paid only a million lire for it, or at least so he claims. From what I can gather it is a tower that is collapsing and it must be full of brambles and snakes. Your father has got it into his head to install countless baths and toilets. He continued to talk on the phone in his croaking voice and simply gestured to Matilde with his hand. Matilde reacted haughtily and began to leaf through a picture magazine. When he hung up, your father told Matilde that he thought she was much fatter. Then he immediately brought up something that happened three years ago when Matilde had given him the manuscript of her novel titled *Polenta and Poison* to read and he had forgotten it in a bar in the station in Florence. It was the only corrected and retyped copy and was in a blue folder. Matilde wrote to the bar but the blue folder was never found. So she gave up correcting her copy and retyping it again because she was discouraged and disappointed. Your father's having left the blue folder in that bar seemed to her an act of contempt. Then, they fought about the vineyard they own jointly near Spoleto. She wanted to sell; your father did not. Anyway, the day before yesterday your father said he was sorry to have lost the blue folder but that *Polenta and Poison* was a silly novel and it was better buried for good. Then he had an attack of nausea and pain. The architect—the one who is doing the tower—came, but your father didn't feel like looking at tiles and deciding whether he liked those with the little blue flower or those with the little brown flower. The architect is something like 6½ feet tall. To me he seems stupid. He looked utterly bewildered. We told him to come back later. So he stuffed the tiles in his brief case, grabbed his raincoat, and rushed out.

You must write me right away because I need to know your permanent address. I am thinking of sending some clothes and money for you with someone who is coming to London. I will find someone. Meanwhile I will write you at this address. I will send you news of your father. I will tell him that you had to leave in a hurry because the registration at the sculpture school was about to close. Anyway, he considers you a person of great foresight. Everything you do always seems to him the only right thing ever done.

I got the rabbits, four of them. I have called a carpenter to make the hutch. I knew I couldn't expect this small favor from you. I realize that maybe it's not your fault. But things always work out so that I have to do without even a little help from you.

Mother

4

London, December 3, 1970

Dear Angelica,

I left in a hurry because they telephoned in the middle of the night to tell me that Anselmo had been arrested. I called you from the airport but didn't get you.

I am sending this letter with a boy who will deliver it by hand to you. His name is Ray and I met him here. He comes from Ostend. He is trustworthy. Put him up if you can. He has to stop in Rome for a few days.

You must go immediately to my place. Use some excuse to get Oswald to give you the keys. Tell him you have to look for a book. Tell him anything you want. I almost forgot to tell you that you ought to take a suitcase or bag with you. Inside my stove there is a dismantled submachine gun wrapped in a towel. When leaving, I completely forgot about it, which will seem odd to you, but that is what happened. A friend of mine named Oliviero brought it to me one evening several weeks ago because he was afraid the police would search his place. I told him to stick it in the stove. I never lit that stove. It is wood-burning. I never had wood. Anyway, after that I completely forgot about the existence of this gun in my stove. Suddenly I remembered it on the plane. There I was in the open sky. I broke into a steaming sweat. It is not true that fear causes a cold sweat. Sometimes it is boiling. I had to take off my sweater. So get that submachine gun and stick it in a bag or suitcase you bring with you. Give it to someone above suspicion. Your cleaning woman, for example. Or you can return it to Oliviero. His name is Oliviero Marzullo. I don't know his address, but get it from someone. However, now that I think about it, the machine gun is so old and rusted that maybe you could throw it in the Tiber. I don't want to give this job to Oswald. I prefer to ask you. In fact, I would prefer that Oswald knows nothing about it. I don't want to be thought a total imbecile. But if you get the urge to tell Oswald about this, go ahead and tell him. I couldn't care less if he thinks I'm an imbecile.

Of course, my passport had expired. Of course, Oswald helped me get it renewed. All in a few hours. Gianni was also at the airport and we had a fight because he suspects there is a Fascist spy in our group, perhaps more than one. I am sure he is imagining this. Gianni is not leaving Rome. He will simply sleep in a different place every night.

Before I left, I stopped to see our father for a minute. Oswald was waiting for me in the car. Father was sound asleep. He seemed to me very old and very sick.

I am O.K. I have a long narrow room with torn draperies. The entire place is long and narrow. There is a hall and all the bedrooms are along this hall. There are five in the boardinghouse. It costs four pounds a week. The owner is a Rumanian Jewess who sells face cream.

When you can, go and see a girl I know in Via dei Prefetti. I don't remember the number. Oswald knows it. The name of this girl is Mara Castorelli. She has had a baby. I gave her money for an abortion, but she didn't have the abortion. The baby could be my son since I slept with her a few times. But she slept with lots of men. Take her some money if you can.

Michael

Angelica read this letter as she sprawled in an armchair in the dining room of her home. It was a tiny and very dark dining room, almost completely filled by a table loaded with books, papers, and a typewriter with a flickering lamp over it. Oreste, her husband, worked at the table but now he was asleep in the bedroom because he worked nights at the newspaper and usually slept until four in the afternoon. The kitchen door was open, and she could see her little girl Flora and her friend Sonia and the young man who had delivered the letter. Her little girl was eating bread dunked in Ovaltine. She was a bright little thing of five dressed in a blue jumper and red tights. Her friend Sonia was a tall, stooped, gentle young woman with glasses and a long black ponytail. She was washing the dishes from the evening before. The young man was eating some warmed-up pasta with tomato sauce left over from Oreste's supper of the night before. He wore a faded blue windbreaker that he did not want to take off because he had caught cold during the trip. His chestnut-colored beard was short and sparse.

Having read the letter, Angelica got up from the chair and searched for her shoes on the rug. She wore dark-green tights and she, too, had on a blue jumper that was rather rumpled and messy because she had been wearing it since the previous day and night, which she had spent at the hospital. Her father had been operated on the day before and had died during the night.

Angelica piled up her long light blonde hair and pinned it in a mass on the top of her head. She was twenty-three, a tall pale young woman with a somewhat over-long face, green eyes like her mother's but more elongated and narrower. She took a bag of flowered black cloth from a closet. She did not have to ask Oswald for the keys to the basement apartment because he had already given them to her; she was supposed to pick up the dirty laundry and take it to be washed. She had the keys in the pocket of her fake fur coat bought secondhand at Porta Portese. She called into the kitchen that she was going to do the marketing and went out.

Her car was parked in front of the Chiesa Nuova. Once in the car she remained motionless for a minute. Then she drove toward Farnese Square. She recalled having seen her father one October day on Via dei Giubbonari. He was walking toward her with his big stride, both hands in his pockets. His long black uncombed hair, tie flapping, black alpaca jacket very wrinkled as always, his large dark-skinned face with its wide mouth set in an expression of bitterness and distaste. She was coming out of a movie theater with her little girl. He gave her a soft, indifferent, perspiring hand. For a number of years they had stopped embracing. Since they met rarely, they did not have much to say to one another. They drank some coffee standing in an espresso bar. He bought the child a large pastry filled with cream. She suggested that it might be stale. He took offense, saying that he came here frequently and the pastries were never stale. A friend of his lived downstairs, he explained, an Irish girl who played the cello. While they were drinking their coffee, the girl appeared—plump, not pretty, and a nose with an odd slant to it. They went to look at coats because the girl wanted a coat. They went into a clothing store on Paradiso Square. The girl began to try on coats. Angelica's father bought her little girl a poncho embroidered with designs of goats. The Irish girl chose a long coat of black reindeer lined with white fur and was very happy. Angelica's father pulled a handful of dirty bills from his pocket and paid. A corner of his handkerchief remained sticking out of his pocket. He always had a corner of his handkerchief hanging out of his pocket. Then they all went to the Medusa gallery where he was supervising the hanging of an exhibition that was to open a few days later. The owners of the gallery, two young men in leather jackets, were busily writing the invitations for the opening. Almost all the paintings were already hung, among them a large portrait of Angelica's mother, painted many years ago when her mother and father still lived together. It showed her mother at a window with her hands folded under her chin. She was wearing a blue-and-white striped blouse. Her hair was a cloud of blazing red. The face was triangular, thin, lined and with a mocking expression. The heavy-lidded eyes were languid and scornful. Angelica remembered that when that portrait was painted they were living in their house in Pieve di Cadore. She recognized the window and the green awnings over the terrace. Later, the house was sold. With his hands in his pockets, her father stopped before the picture and praised the colors, which he defined as biting and cruel. Then he set about praising every one of his pictures in the gallery. Recently, he had started painting enormous canvases in which he jumbled together all kinds of objects. He had discovered the technique of the jumble. Ships, automobiles, bicycles, motorboats, dolls, soldiers, cemeteries, nude women, and dead animals swayed in a greenish light. In his bitter croaking voice he said that nobody else today was up to painting with such scope and such exactitude. His pictures were tragic, splendid, gigantic and meticulously detailed. He said "my pictures," rolling the "r" with a pained lonely anger. Angelica thought that neither she nor the Irish girl nor the owners of the gallery nor perhaps even her father himself believed a word that croaking voice was saying. The voice droned on with the grating solitary sound of a broken record. Suddenly, Angelica remembered a song her father used to sing while he painted. "*Non avemo ni canones—ni tanks ni aviones—oi*

Carmelà!" She asked him if he still sang *"Oi Carmelà!"* while painting. Unexpectedly he seemed touched. He said, no, he didn't sing anything any more because his new paintings required so much effort. He had to paint standing up on a ladder and sweated so much he had to change his shirt every two hours. All of a sudden he seemed anxious to get rid of the Irish girl. He said it was getting dark and it would be better for her to go home. He could not see her home because he had a dinner engagement. The Irish girl got into a taxi. He spoke angrily about the girl's always taking taxis although she came from some wretched place in Ireland where there was nothing but fog, peat, sheep, and certainly no taxis. He took Angelica by the arm and walked her and the little girl toward Via dei Banchi Vecchi where they lived. Then he began to complain about everyone. He was alone. He had a stupid servant whom he had recently fished out of an electrical repair shop. No one came to visit him. He almost never saw the twins who anyway had grown too fat recently. They each weighed 127 pounds at only fourteen years of age. Two hundred and fifty-four pounds between them was too much weight, he said. He almost never saw Viola, whom he couldn't abide anyway because she lacked a sense of humor. A completely humorless person. She had settled down with her husband in the home of her in-laws. There were lots of people in that house, in-laws, uncles, grandchildren. They were a real tribe. They didn't amount to much. Pharmacists. Of course, he said, as he went into a pharmacy, he didn't have anything against pharmacies. He bought some Alka-Seltzer because he always had a vague pain "here" he said, pointing to the center of his chest. Maybe it was his old ulcer, that good old lifelong friend. Then, as to Michael, he saw little of him recently and that saddened him. When Michael went to live on his own, he had thought it right though sad. Speaking of Michael, his voice ceased croaking and became thin and subdued. But now Michael was always with Oswald. He couldn't figure out what sort of person that Oswald was. No doubt he was very kind, polite, retiring. Michael used to drag him along when he came to Via San Sebastianello with his pile of dirty laundry. Probably he found Oswald useful since Oswald had a car and could drive him around. Michael no longer had a car. He had lost his license when he ran into an old nun. He killed her but it was not his fault. He was entirely blameless. He had just learned to drive and he was hurrying to his mother, who had called him because she felt depressed. His mother felt depressed often. She couldn't bear to be alone, he said, lowering his voice to a rasping whisper, and in her complete stupidity she didn't realize that that fellow Cavalieri had been on the verge of leaving her for some time. She was naïve. She had the mind of a teen-age girl in spite of her forty-four years. Forty-two, Angelica said. Quite soon forty-three. He made a rapid calculation on his fingers and continued talking. She was more naïve than the twins. Besides, the twins were not at all naïve. They were as cold and sly as two vixens. And that Cavalieri had always seemed to him a worthless fellow. He hadn't ever liked him, what with those drooping shoulders, those long white fingers, those little curls. He had the profile of a sparrow. Her father claimed to be an expert at spotting sparrows. At the doorway of the apartment house where Angelica lived he said he didn't want to come in because he disliked Oreste, her husband. He considered him a pedant, a moralizer. He kissed neither Angelica nor the little girl. He gave the child a pat on the nape of her neck and grasped Angelica by both arms. He advised her to come to the opening the next day. That show would be "a big thing," he said. He walked away. Angelica did not go to the opening the next day because she went with her husband to Naples where he had a meeting. She saw her father two or three times after that. He was sick in bed and her mother was there. He never spoke to her.

One time he was telephoning. Another time he felt ill and greeted her with a weak disgusted gesture of his hand.

Angelica went down the six steps that led to the basement apartment, entered, and turned on the light. Against one wall of the room was an unmade bed. Angelica recognized the pretty blankets that her mother used to buy, soft blankets in pastel colors, bordered in velvet, and light and warm. Her mother enjoyed buying pretty blankets. The floor was littered with empty bottles, newspapers, and paintings. She glanced at the pictures of vultures, owls, houses in ruins. Under the window there was a heap of dirty laundry, a pair of jeans, a teapot, an ashtray full of butts, and a bowl of oranges. The stove stood in the center of the room. It was a large pot-bellied stove of green tile decorated with delicate designs resembling embroidery. Angelica stuck her arm in and fished out a bundle wrapped in an old terry cloth towel with a fringe. She put it in her shopping bag along with the dirty laundry and the oranges. She left the apartment and pulling up the collar of her coat to cover her mouth she went into the humid foggy morning. After walking two blocks she stopped at a laundry that called itself "The Rapid" and waited while they counted the laundry piece by piece. Then she got back in the car. She drove to Lungotevere Ripa slowly because of the traffic. She went down the steps that led to the river's edge and hurled the bundle into the river. A boy asked her what she had thrown in. She replied that she had thrown away some rotten oranges.

"*Non avemo ni canones—ni tanks ni aviones,*" she sang as she drove home through the traffic. Suddenly she noticed that her face was wet with tears. She laughed, sobbed, and dried the tears on the sleeve of her coat. Near home she stopped to buy a loin of pork that she planned to braise along with potatoes. She also bought two bottles of beer and a box of sugar. Then she bought a black scarf and a pair of black stockings to wear at her father's funeral.

5

Dear Mother,

For reasons that I can't easily explain in a letter, I decided after a moment of indecision not to come to Rome. When Oswald telephoned me that Father had died, I went to see what flights there were for Rome, but then I didn't leave. I know you told all the relatives that I had pneumonia. Good.

Thanks for the clothes and the money. The person who brought them, the nephew of Mrs. Schlitz, gave me no news of you because he doesn't know you but he did give me some news of Oswald and gave me back my watch, which I had left in Oswald's pocket when I went to take a shower in a rush that day at the airport. Give Oswald my thanks. I haven't time to write him directly.

I am leaving London and going to Sussex. I am going to the home of a professor of glottology. I am supposed to wash the dishes, light the furnace, and walk the dogs. For the moment I have given up the idea of going to school to study sculpture. I prefer dogs and dishes.

I am sorry I didn't make that hutch for your rabbits, but I will do it when I return. Kisses to you and my sisters.

Michael

6

December 8, 1970

Dear Michael,

Mission accomplished with regard to that little object forgotten in your stove. I threw it in the Tiber since it was, as you said, rusted.

On the other hand, I did not go to see the girl in Via dei Prefatti. I haven't had the time. My little girl has a cold. Also, you asked me to take that girl some money and at the moment, I don't have any.

Our father was buried three days ago. I will write you at greater length as soon as I can.

Angelica

7

December 12, 1970

Dear Michael

I just received your brief letter. I don't know what kept you from returning when your father died. I can't imagine how anyone could be kept from coming in case of such a misfortune. I just don't understand it. I wonder if you will come when I die. Yes, we told the various relatives that you were in London with pneumonia.

I am glad you are going to Sussex. The air must be very good there, and I am always glad to know that you are out in the country. When you children were small, it used to bore me to death to stay in the country for months on end. I thought that every day spent there was good for all of you. Later when you went to live with your father, I drove myself crazy because he frequently kept you in Rome at the height of the summer. He didn't like the country; he only liked the seashore. He used to send you to Ostia in the morning with the maid and he insisted it worked out very well.

You don't say whether or not you have to cook for this professor of glottology. Write and tell me if you have to cook and I will send you some recipes. Matilde keeps a large notebook in which she pastes all the recipes she finds in newspapers and on calendars.

You give me your telephone number in Sussex but I would have to call you from the public phone because they still have not installed my telephone. The public phone is in a tavern that is always crowded. I am afraid if I call you, I will begin to cry. That tavern is no place for telephoning and crying.

Your father's death was a severe blow. Now I feel much more alone. He was no help to me because he was not interested in me or even in your sisters. He cared only about you. His affection focused on a person whom he had invented and who didn't resemble you at all. I can't explain to you why I feel more alone since his death. Maybe because we shared certain memories. We were the only people in the world who shared those memories. It is true that we never referred to them when we met. However, now I realize that it wasn't necessary to talk about them. We were aware of them during those hours spent at Canova, hours which I found so oppressive and interminable. They were not happy memories because your father and I had never been very happy together. And even the brief rare moments of happiness we did share were dirtied and trampled on later. However, one loves not just the happy memories. At a certain point in life, one is aware that one simply loves one's memories.

You will think it strange, but I will never be able to go back to Canova because if I went I would begin to sob like an idiot. If I am certain of one thing it is that I don't want to let people see me cry.

We have dismissed that Henry or Frederick, I never could remember his name, who worked for your father. Ada, Oswald's wife, has taken him on. According to Matilde, I should have hired him but I didn't want him because he is stupid. According to Oswald, Ada will teach him all kinds of things, since she seems to have a talent for training domestics and making them into impeccable and impenetrable beings. I don't know how she will render impeccable that insipid and squint-eyed young man who looks like a wild boar, but Oswald says that Ada's art is boundless when it comes to sublimation of domestics.

Every day Matilde and I go to Via San Sebastianello to put your father's papers in order and we are numbering the paintings that we will eventually put in storage. We don't know what to do with the furniture, which is all enormous and heavy. Neither Viola nor Angelica had any room. That is why we are thinking of selling it. Yesterday Oswald and that cousin of your father's, Lillino, came to see the paintings. Lillino left today for Mantova, and I am glad because I can't bear him. Lillino advises against selling the paintings now because at this moment your father's pictures bring very little. The most recent ones are enormous and frankly I think they are horrible. I gathered that Oswald also finds them ugly. I understood this even though he looked at them without saying a word. On the other hand, Lillino says they are magnificent and that tomorrow the public will discover them and they will be worth a fortune. Matilde merely tosses her forelock and smacks her lips to express her admiration. I can't look at them because I get dizzy. Who knows why he began to paint those enormous cluttered pictures. I have kept for myself that portrait of me at the window of the house in Pieve di Cadore done many years ago. A few months later your father sold the house. I have hung the portrait in the living room and I can look at it as I write to you. Of all your father's paintings this one is dearest to me. We separated shortly after it was painted when we returned to Rome at the end of the summer. At that time we lived on Trieste Boulevard. You and Viola and Angelica were at Chianciano with Aunt

Cecilia. Maybe your sisters were aware of what was about to happen, but you were not because you were little, only six years old. One morning I left the house on Trieste Boulevard and I left it for good. I took the twins and joined my parents who were vacationing at Roccadimezzo. I arrived at Roccadimezzo after an indescribable trip with the twins, who threw up the entire time on the bus. My parents were staying quietly in a good hotel where they could enjoy the food and go for short walks in the meadows. They did not expect me because I had not notified them. I arrived at the hotel late in the evening with three suitcases and the twins covered with vomit. When my parents saw me, they were terribly upset. I hadn't slept for a week because of the emotional uncertainty and anguish and I must have looked awful. Two months later my mother had her first heart attack. I have always thought that she suffered that heart attack from the shock of seeing me arrive at Roccadimezzo that evening in such a state. In the spring my mother died of the second attack.

Your father had decreed that you were to stay with him. You with him and the girls with me. He bought the house in Via San Sebastianello and installed himself there with you. He had an old cook, but she stayed on only a few months. I don't remember her name. Maybe you do. For a long time I could not so much as put a foot in that house because he didn't want to see me. I used to telephone you and you would cry on the phone. I have a terrible remembrance of this. I used to wait with the twins for you in the park of the Villa Borghese, and you came there with the old cook who wore a wrap of monkey fur. At first, when the cook told you it was time to go home, you would set up a howl and throw yourself on the ground but later on you took your scooter and went off with a calm, set expression on your face. I can still see you in your little overcoat walking away quickly and firmly. I had built up such a hatred of your father that I thought of going into the house on Via San Sebastianello with a pistol and shooting him. Perhaps a mother should not tell a son these things because they are not very edifying and educational. But nobody knows what a good upbringing is any more or if there is really such a thing. I didn't bring you up. I wasn't there, so how could I. The only times I saw you were on those occasional afternoons in the park of the Villa Borghese. Your father certainly didn't give you any sort of discipline, since he was determined to believe that you were born with perfect manners. So no one gave you any training at all. You grew up very scatterbrained but I am not sure that you would have been less so if you had received any training from us. Maybe your sisters are less scatterbrained than you. But they, too, are certainly odd and scatterbrained, each in her own fashion. Certainly, I didn't provide any education in the home then and I don't now. The reason is that I often felt and still feel that I dislike the person I am. One has to have a little faith and liking for oneself in order to raise and teach someone else.

I don't remember when or how your father and I stopped hating each other. Once in the lawyer's office he slapped me so hard that I had a nosebleed. His cousin Lillino was present. He and the lawyer made me lie on the sofa and Lillino went out to get some absorbent cotton. Your father locked himself in the bathroom and wouldn't come out. He is afraid of blood and he felt sick. I see that I have written "he is." I never remember that he is dead. Lillino and the lawyer pounded on the bathroom door. He came out looking pale and with his hair dripping wet because he had stuck his head under the faucet. When I think back on this scene I want to laugh. Many times later I wanted to remind him of it and laugh about it with him. But our relationship had petrified. We could no longer laugh together. It seems to me that he stopped hating me after that slap. He still didn't want me to come to Via San Sebastianello but sometimes he brought you to the park. I, too, had stopped hating him. One time in the park we played blind-man's-bluff with you children. I fell down and he wiped the mud off my dress with his handkerchief. While he was bending over to wipe away the mud, I saw his head with its long black locks and I understood that there wasn't even a shadow of hatred left. That was a moment of happiness, a happiness based on nothing because I knew perfectly well that my relationship with your father would continue to be abject and despicable even though free of hatred. Still, I recall that the sun was setting and there were great red clouds over the city and I felt almost peaceful and almost happy.

I have nothing to tell you about your father's death. Matilde and I visited him in the hospital the day before. He chatted, argued with Matilde, called the architect on the telephone and talked about the tower. He said he had bought the tower primarily for you because you love the seashore and you could spend entire summers there in the tower. You could invite all your friends, since there would be a lot of bedrooms. I know you don't like the sea and that you are quite capable of sitting on the beach completely dressed and sweating in mid-August. However, I didn't want to contradict him so I didn't reply. He continued to fantasize about the tower. According to him it was a real bargain; the purchase was a stroke of genius. He said he was given to such strokes of genius frequently and it was too bad that I had no such talent because the house I bought for myself must be a very ugly, badly designed and expensive house. I did not reply. Then a group of his friends arrived. They telephoned from downstairs. He said he was tired and did not want to see Biagioni, Casalis, Maschera, and an Irish girl who I think was his mistress. I sent Matilde out to receive them. So he and I remained alone together. He told me that I could spend the summer in the tower. However, he didn't want the twins because they would bring their radios and disturb his afternoon nap. I told him he was unfair to the twins because if you came to the tower with a gang of your friends I didn't think he would get any sleep in the afternoon. Then he said that maybe sometime he would invite the twins, but definitely not Viola and Angelica. Viola could visit her in-laws at their place in that ugly fly-ridden countryside. She should amuse herself there. Angelica had her tiresome husband, Oreste. Did she love him? Perhaps, but he wouldn't have Oreste at the tower because once that fool had criticized Cézanne. He was a frog. How dare such a frog brain have opinions about Cézanne. He planned to pick his guests carefully every summer. And not only in the summer because he intended to live in the tower all year round. Matilde would definitely not be invited. He had never been able to abide her, not even as a child. He could not understand why I had dragged her into my house. I said I felt lonely and needed company. I preferred Matilde to no one, and I felt sorry for Matilde who no longer had a cent. Your father said she could always sell that vineyard. I reminded him that they had sold the vineyard some time ago, sold it for a pittance and now a motel stood on the site. He said I was nasty to remind him of this. He turned onto his other side and didn't want to talk any more. He didn't even speak with Matilde again. Then Matilde told me that the Irish girl was in tears and Biagioni and Casalis had dragged her away.

They operated on your father at eight in the morning. We were all there in the waiting room, I, Matilde, Angelica, Viola, Elio, and Oreste. The twins stayed at the house of a friend. The operation did not take very long. Afterward I learned that they had simply cut him open and sewn him up without doing anything because there was nothing to be done. Matilde and I stayed in the room. Angelica and Viola stayed outside in the waiting room. He didn't speak again and died at two o'clock that night.

There were lots of people at the funeral. Biagioni spoke

first, then Maschera. Your father couldn't bear either Biagioni or Maschera. He said they did not understand his new style of painting. He said they envied him, that they were sparrows. He said he had always known how to spot sparrows.

I see that you don't read my letters, or you read and immediately forget them. You can't make the rabbit hutch when you return because I have already had it made by a carpenter. I have four rabbits, four of them, but I don't know if I will stay here in the country for much longer. I am not at all sure that I don't loathe this place.

Philip came to your father's funeral.

Fondly,

Mother

Having finished and sealed this letter, Adriana put on a camel-hair coat and covered her head with a black wool scarf. It was five o'clock in the afternoon. She went into the kitchen and looked in the refrigerator. She looked with disgust at the beef tongue that Matilde had left to marinate in a salad bowl. They would be afflicted for months on end by that tongue probably marinated badly. Neither Matilde nor the twins were at home. Cloti was in bed with the flu. Adriana went to the doorway of her room. Cloti, dressed in a bathrobe, lay under the covers. She had wrapped her head in a towel. The twins' radio was on the night table. Adriana told her to take her temperature. She waited. Bobby Solo was singing. Cloti said she adored Bobby Solo. It was the first time Adriana had heard her speak openly and pleasantly. Cloti's words were usually accompanied by sighs and dealt with her personal labors, the lumps in her mattress, the cold drafts from the windows. Adriana said she was sorry she could not bring the television set into the room, but it was too heavy to move. Cloti said she didn't care about afternoon TV but she liked it in the evening. She didn't have a television set in her room in her previous job, although there was every other convenience and comfort. She enumerated these: a large attractive room, white and gold furniture and a rug so beautiful that she worried about having it in her room. The mattress was soft and central heating kept the entire house at an even temperature. Her employer, the lawyer, traveled constantly so she had only the cat to care for. Adriana read the thermometer: 97° F. Cloti said she was sure her fever was rising because she felt hot one minute, chilled the next and had a strange headache. Adriana asked if she would like a cup of tea. Cloti said no, but there was one thing about that job with the lawyer that she didn't like. When he was home, the lawyer wanted her to sit and talk with him in the living room in the evening. She didn't know what to talk about. Not that the lawyer had ever made any advances. He understood and respected her. He only wanted conversation. That was why she left. She didn't feel like conversing. And, of course, there was gossip. When the lawyer's sister came for a visit she made some unfavorable comments about the cooking. Once the sister told her to take a bath because she smelled. That, of course, was untrue because she washed her feet and under her arms every morning. She took a bath only once a month because baths made her weak. Anyway, those were only excuses. Gossip was behind it all. Now, however, she realized she had made a mistake to quit, an enormous mistake.

Adriana left the house and took the car out of the garage. She opened the gate. She loathed the two miniature firs Matilde had had planted on either side of the gate. They stood in that empty garden with their fake alpine air. She hoped they would die. The road curved sharply through the countryside. The car bounced. The day had been very sunny and there was little snow left. The sunlight still outlined the town and hilltops but dusk had already spread over the plain with a cold gray mist. She hated the twins for not coming home. She hated Matilde who had gone to buy olives and capers for the tongue. The countryside was deserted for a long stretch but then a low cottage appeared. A thread of smoke came out of a pipe in one of the windows. Two photographers lived there. At that moment the man could be seen washing dishes in a blue plastic pail and the woman wearing a red coat and torn stockings was hanging the laundry on the line. Somehow the sight of those two people gave her an acute feeling of despair. They seemed to her the only beings which the universe afforded her. For another long stretch there was nothing but mud, withered hedges and empty fields, but finally the road joined the highway and a continuous stream of traffic. On the edge of the highway workmen in coveralls gathered around a drum of tar.

She thought of Philip's wife, whom she had seen at the funeral wearing a yellow coat fastened over her pregnant stomach by two large tortoise shell buttons. Her young face was hard and thin. Her hair was drawn back into a small smooth bun. Rosy-cheeked, serious, she walked next to Philip, carrying a small purse in her hand. Philip was the same as ever. He put his glasses on and off, ran his long fingers through his coarse gray curls. He looked about with an expression of false determination and authority. The road into the town rose to the crest of a hill and from there on was illuminated with big street lights. The lamp posts were hung with paper garlands in preparation for a parade. She mailed the letter in town and bought some eggs from a woman seated with a basket and a brazier in front of the church. She talked with the woman about the sudden wind that drove black clouds over the roofs and whipped the paper garlands. She went to the public phone and called Angelica, covering one ear to cut out the noise. She invited her to Sunday dinner. They would have tongue. The connection was bad and Angelica did not understand. They said good-bye and she got back in her car. The day Philip had come to tell her he was getting married, he came with Angelica. He wanted Angelica with him for fear she would cry hysterically. He was stupid. She rarely cried. She stood up to everything. She was solid as an oak. And after all she had expected it for sometime, but from that day on she detested the house in Via dei Villini because she had remained stretched out in that bedroom with the arched ceiling and wept a little when Philip left and Angelica held her hand.

8

"She seems utterly stupid to me," Ada said.

"Not utterly," Oswald said.

"Yes, utterly," Ada said.

"Not stupid, just scatterbrained," Oswald said.

"I fail to see the distinction," Ada said.

"Well, she can boil a couple of eggs," Oswald said. "I know Mrs. Schlitz's mother. She is a person of simple tastes."

"It is not just a matter of boiled eggs," said Ada. "I know old Mrs. Schlitz better than you do. She is not easily satisfied. She wants her house in order, the floors waxed. I don't see that one waxing floors. Furthermore, the baby's crying will annoy the old lady."

"I didn't know how to help her and I felt sorry for her with that baby," Oswald said.

"And so you dumped her on the Schlitzes."

"The Schlitzes love babies."

"Yes, babies they see in carriages in the park, not those that scream at night in their own house."

Oswald had lunched at Ada's and now they sat in the living room. He pasted stamps in an album for Elisabeth. Ada knitted. Elisabeth was on the porch with a friend. They were sitting on the floor playing cards very silently and seriously.

"It is pointless to paste those stamps," Ada said. "She is quite able to do it herself and besides she enjoys doing it."

Oswald closed the album with a rubber band and went to look out onto the porch, which was enclosed with glass and filled with house plants. He knocked on the glass but Elisabeth was too absorbed in her game to raise her head.

"That azalea has done wonderfully," he said.

"You know I have a green thumb. It's nothing new. That plant looked dead when it arrived here. It had been in Michael's father's house. His servant brought it to me. They were about to throw it out. It was his idea to bring it here."

"So he does think sometimes."

"Sometimes. Not often. But he is not unwilling. I taught him to wait at table. Did you notice how well he waits at table?"

Oswald was about to say, "You also have a green thumb with butlers," but then he thought the words might have a kind of sexual double meaning so he said nothing but blushed just the same.

"On the other hand, that girl of yours will never learn anything," Ada said.

"She doesn't have to wait on table at the Schlitzes. They all three eat in the kitchen."

"What has she done with that apartment where she was staying in Via dei Prefetti?"

"Nothing. She goes there Sundays. She leaves the baby at the Schlitzes and she goes to Via dei Prefetti. She rests there and a girl friend visits her."

"She probably goes to bed with someone there."

"Maybe. I don't know. She says she is tired of sleeping

around. The only thing that interests her now is the baby. She has stopped nursing him. She feeds him his bottles."

"That means Mrs. Schlitz senior feeds him."

"I guess so."

"That baby looks a lot like Michael. I am sure it's his," Ada said.

"Do you think so?"

"Yes. It's Michael all over."

"The baby has black hair. Michael's is reddish."

"Hair doesn't count. The mouth, the expression count. I think Michael should come back here and recognize it as his. He would if he had any decency, which he hasn't. He would not have to marry the girl, because one doesn't marry a type like that, just give the baby his name. What are you thinking of doing with that basement apartment?"

"I don't know. You tell me. For the moment I am letting a fellow named Ray, a friend of Michael's from London, sleep there. I think he will leave in a few days."

"I breathed a sigh of relief when Michael left. Now you have put another one in there."

"He didn't know where to go. He was staying at Angelica's but her husband won't have him in the house any more. They fought over politics. Her husband is very rigid. He won't let anyone question those cast-iron opinions of his."

"If he were so convinced he wouldn't care whether or not his views were challenged. He gets so angry, because his opinions are not of cast iron but of cottage cheese. I know that husband of Angelica's. I find him an insignificant flunky, one of those party hacks who resemble book-keepers."

"You may be right there."

"I have the feeling that Angelica's marriage won't last long. Today no marriages last any length of time. For that matter, our marriage didn't last very long."

"It lasted exactly four years," Oswald said.

"Does that seem long to you, four years?" she asked.

53

"No. I am simply saying it was four years, exactly four."

"Frankly, I don't like these young men who wander around today. They are drifters, dangerous types. I almost prefer the bookkeepers. The apartment as such is not important but it would really annoy me if someone blew it up."

"Also because in that case I would get blown up, too, on the floor above as would the tailor on the top floor," Oswald said. "But I don't think this Ray is the type to blow up anything. He doesn't seem to have discovered gunpowder yet."

"Please don't bring him here. I don't want to meet this Ray. You used to bring Michael here and I didn't like him. He wasn't amusing. He used to sit down and fix me with his little green eyes. I think he thought me an idiot. Anyway, I didn't find him amusing. I put myself out so that he could leave; I helped him but not because I liked him."

"You did it out of kindness," Oswald said.

"Yes and because I was glad not to see him any more. However, I found it incredible that he didn't come back when his father died. Incredible."

"He was afraid of being arrested," Oswald said. "Two or three in that group have been arrested."

"I still think it is incredible and you did too. You were astounded. One does risk arrest in order to accompany the mortal remains of one's father to the cemetery."

"The mortal remains?" Oswald said.

"Yes, the mortal remains. Have I said something odd?"

"It seemed an unusual expression for you."

"It's a very common expression. Anyway, as I was saying, I didn't find Michael amusing. Polite, maybe. He used to play Monopoly with Elisabeth. He helped me paint furniture, but deep inside he thought me a fool. I knew that and it annoyed me."

"Why do you refer to Michael in the past tense?" Oswald asked.

"Because I have the feeling that he won't ever come

back," Ada said. "We won't see him again. He will end up in America, or who knows where. One can't foresee what he will do. The world today is full of such boys who drift aimlessly from one place to another. One can't imagine how they will grow old. It seems as if they won't ever have to grow old; as if they will stay as they are with no home, no family, no working hours, nothing. Just a couple of rags. They have never been young, so how can they grow old. For example, take that girl with the baby. How can she grow old when she is already old. A withered little plant, faded at birth. Not physically but morally. I can't understand how a person like you can waste time with all these withered little plants. I may be wrong but I have a high opinion of you."

"You are mistaken," Oswald said. "You are too optimistic about me."

"I am optimistic by nature, but I can't see any hope for these boys who drift around. I find them unbearable. They create disorder. They seem very sweet, but deep inside they want to blow everyone up."

"In the end it wouldn't be a bad thing," Oswald said. He had put on his raincoat and smoothed down his thin blond hair.

"Would you want Elisabeth blown up, too?"

"Not Elisabeth," Oswald said.

"You ought to send that raincoat to the cleaners," Ada said.

"Sometimes you sound as if you were still my wife," Oswald said. "What you said just now is a wife talking."

"Do you object?"

"No. Why?"

"You are the one who left me. I didn't leave you. However, let's not go into all that again," Ada said. "Besides, you may have been right. Your decision was a wise one. You like living alone. As for me, I feel fine alone. We couldn't live together. We are too different."

"Too different," Oswald said.

"Just don't parrot me. It really irritates me," Ada said. "Now I must go to Elisabeth's school. I promised the teachers I would make the costumes for the puppets in the Christmas play. I am going to bring some scraps of material I have put aside in a trunk."

"You are always inventing chores," Oswald said. "You could stay here quietly the entire afternoon. The weather is bad, not cold but windy."

"If I stayed closed in here all afternoon, I get depressed," Ada said.

"Good-bye," Oswald said.

"Good-bye," Ada said. "Do you want to know something?"

"What?"

"Deep inside, Michael thought that you were a stupid fool, too, not only me. He clung to you like a leech. He used you and secretly he thought you a fool."

"Michael never used me," Oswald said.

He went out. He had left his car in the garage, so he walked onto the bridge and stopped for a moment to watch the dark-yellow waters of the river and the tall plane trees on its banks where the traffic passed. A hot fierce wind was blowing. The sky was overcast with black swollen clouds. Oswald thought of the machine gun that Angelica told him she had thrown in the water not far from that bridge. It occurred to him that he had never in his entire life had a weapon in his hand, not even a gun for underwater fishing. For that matter Michael had never touched a gun as far as he knew. Michael had been exempted from military service because his father had bribed someone to get him off. Oswald as the only son of a widowed mother had been legally exempt. At the time of the Resistance he was a little boy. He and his mother had been evacuees in the vicinity of Varese.

He turned down a narrow side street full of children.

He went into the little shop. Mrs. Schlitz was moving books and limping around on her swollen ankles. She smiled at him.

"How are you?" he said.

"She has gone back to Via dei Prefetti," she said. "It was impossible to keep her. She was no help in the house. In fact, my mother ended up cooking for her. When she took a shower, she didn't dry herself properly, so there were footprints all over the house. The other day when my mother and I were out, she left without her door key, leaving the baby at home alone. The poor little thing was crying and the superintendent's wife couldn't find a locksmith so she called the fire department. In order to get in, the firemen had to break a window. My mother had grown fond of the baby, but that girl went out often and left him so my mother had to change and feed him."

"I'm sorry," Oswald said. "I will pay for the window."

"That doesn't matter. We would have been very glad to keep her with us and it would have been a kind thing to do but she has no sense at all. She used to wake us up at night to help her change the baby. She said it depressed her to do it alone. She woke us both, my mother and me, because she said the more people around the better. We felt sorry for her. Still, one can't understand why she wanted to have that baby, when she finds it so painfully difficult to take care of him."

"True. One can't understand it," Oswald said. "And yet one can understand it very well."

"She left today. We put the baby in the yellow plastic carrier and covered him well so he wouldn't catch cold. We called her a taxi. My mother had to lend her a sweater because she didn't have anything warm. She burned that coat with the dragons while ironing it."

"What a shame," Oswald said.

"Yes. It was a nice coat. Very becoming. She left the hot iron on it when she went to the telephone. She chatted for a long time with someone on the phone. She said later it was Angelica. The iron burned a large mark on the back, right where the dragons were. In another few minutes the whole ironing board would have caught fire. My mother was terribly frightened. I worry about my mother. She is old and she was getting so tired and frightened. If I had had only myself to think about, I might have kept her on."

"I understand. I am sorry," Oswald said.

9

December 18, 1970

Dear Michael,

I have seen the girl in Via dei Prefetti. Mara. What a comic-strip name. Maria would have been better. An "i" could have made a difference.

I took her some money that I got from Mother. However, Oswald says that rather than giving her money we must help her find some sort of job, which is not a simple matter since she is unable to do anything. Oswald had arranged for her to stay with Mrs. Schlitz. It seems that there is a Mrs. Schlitz senior, eighty years old but lively, and they live on Montesacro. Mara was supposed to help a little in the house. They took her in with the baby and gave her some money every month. However, shortly thereafter she set the house on fire and they had to call the fire department. At least, this is what I gathered from a long confused story she told me. She also said there was very little to eat, a piece of dried cod at lunch and the same thing reheated with onions at supper. She couldn't digest it and lived on Alka-Seltzer. She used to wake up at night ravenously hungry and would wander about the house looking for cheese. So her milk dried up. However, Oswald says this girl lies. The baby is cute but he is not yours. He has an enormous mouth and long black hair, which of course he might have inherited from our father. Now she and the baby are back in Via dei Prefetti.

Ray, that boy you sent, stayed at my place for a week but he fought with Oreste and once called him a "revisionist," at which point Oreste became so furious that he punched him in the mouth. He began to bleed. I was afraid his teeth had been broken but only his lip had been cut. Sonia, Ray, and I went to the drugstore. Oreste stayed at home. He was very upset. Ray was not upset. However, the lip bled so much that his windbreaker was all stained. The pharmacist said it was only a cut and put a Band-Aid on it. The next day I called Oswald, and now Ray is living in your basement apartment. Sonia brings him food and comic books to read because he wants to learn how to write and draw comics. He has a friend who works for a comic-book publisher and has promised to introduce him to the editor. So he spends his time trying to draw women with enormous breasts and eyes. He saw your owls and he drew a few owls fluttering around the breasts.

Mother has decided that Oreste punched him out of jealousy. However, Oreste had no cause to be jealous because there is absolutely nothing between Ray and me. He is neither likable nor unlikable. He is an amoeba. Oreste thinks he has Fascist sympathies but then Oreste sees Fascists and spies everywhere. I repeat there is nothing between Ray and me. He sleeps with Sonia in your apartment in your bed with Mother's pretty blankets. I told Mother this and she said to remove those blankets and substitute them with old ones. I don't think I will because it seems such a mean thing to do. At times Mother is mean, usually toward people she has never seen. If she met Ray she wouldn't like the idea of his sleeping under ugly old blankets. I washed Ray's windbreaker, thinking it could be hand washed but that was a mistake because it dried as stiff as a piece of cod.

I went to have Sunday lunch with Mother. Oreste did not come because he had to go to a meeting of trade union leaders. I took my little girl and Oswald was there with his daughter. Mother has some rabbits. The children amused themselves with the rabbits, although I can't imagine how because they are very boring sleepy rabbits. The twins took them out of the hutch, grabbing them by the ears and put them on the grass but they didn't run away. They are a type of rabbit that sheds, and the twins spend hours brushing fur off their clothes. It was a beautiful sunny day. However, Mother seemed very down.

I think Father's death depresses her and sets her thinking back over those years when they were together. Every other minute she is on the verge of crying and then she gets up and goes to another room. She has put that portrait father did of her seated at the window of the house in Pieve di Cadore in the living room. You don't remember that time because you were little, but I recall everything. It was a dreadful summer. They no longer fought but there was an air of tension, a feeling that something was about to happen. Sometimes I heard Mother crying at night.

I didn't know or think about who was right and who was wrong. Then I knew only that waves of misery flowed from their room throughout the house. It was everywhere, in every corner. We had had great fun in that house for many summers. It was a lovely house with many places to play, a woodshed, lots of hiding places. There were turkeys in the courtyard. You don't remember. Then Cecilia came and we went to Chianciano with her. After some weeks our father came and told us that they were separating. He said you would be with him and we girls with Mother. There were no explanations. They had decided. He stayed on at

Chianciano for two or three days. He would sit in the lobby of the hotel smoking and ordering Martinis. When Cecilia spoke to him he would tell her to shut up.

Maybe Mother is still in love with Philip. I don't know. Their relationship lasted so many years and she always expected that he would come and live with her. Instead he married someone younger than I. He didn't have the courage to tell Mother that he was going to marry and he wanted me to be there when he did. Philip is not brave. Anyway, that morning was a horror. It happened last May. I remember it was May because the rose bush under our windows in Via dei Villini was in full bloom.

In fact, Mother is very alone now. The twins pay no attention to her. You aren't there. Viola and I have our own lives. She is there with Matilde who gets on her nerves. However, it is someone, something in the house, a voice, a footstep in those rooms where no one ever goes. Who knows why Mother bought that big house. I think she must regret it now. She must also regret having invited Matilde; nevertheless she knows that total solitude would be worse for her. Still Matilde gets on her nerves. Matilde calls her "dear child" and continually asks, "Are you all right?," caressing her chin and looking into her eyes. Every morning she arrives dressed in her bathing suit to do her yoga in mother's bedroom because she says it is the only really warm room in the house. Mother doesn't have the heart to tell her to leave. Now Mother has become even-tempered. She also has to listen to *Polenta and Poison*, the novel Matilde wrote and has now fished out of her trunk and plans to revise, because Oswald foolishly mentioned that Ada is very close to a certain publisher. His name is Cola-rosa. A small insignificant publisher. I think he may be Ada's lover. Matilde jumped at the idea of this publisher and reads *Polenta and Poison* out loud to Mother and Os-wald every evening. Oswald comes almost every evening. He and Mother have become friends. No sexual implications. Besides, I don't think Oswald is interested in women. I think he is a repressed homosexual and that he is vaguely and unconsciously in love with you. I don't know your thoughts but this is the way I see it.

I wish I could see you. I am all right. Flora goes to kindergarten. She eats at the school and comes home at four. Sonia picks her up because I am in the office until seven. My job becomes more poisonous and stupid daily. Now I am translating a long article on heavy water. When I get home, I have to do the shopping, cook supper, and iron Oreste's shirts because he won't wear drip-dry shirts. Then he goes to work at the paper and I fall asleep in front of the TV.

Love.

Angelica

10

"I think she is terribly stupid," Mara said.

"You are mistaken," said Oswald.

"Terribly," Mara said.

"At times she can be extremely acute and observant. She is limited, that is true, but she is my wife and I wish you would stop calling her stupid."

"You are separated. She is no longer your wife."

"All the same it irritates me when people criticize her in front of me."

"Does that happen often?"

"What do you care?"

"I don't think she is beautiful or chic."

"Actually, she is beautiful and sometimes very elegant."

"She wasn't elegant yesterday, or the time before. She wore the same fur coat. It's North American wolf. The streets are full of these North American wolves. They are all over the place. I couldn't see what sort of figure she has because she kept her coat on. She has good legs but her knees are too big. She wears those big glasses with the tortoise shell frames. She has a slight mustache, bleached, but it's there. She walked around here with her hands in her pockets scrutinizing me, the baby, the apartment. Yesterday when I asked her if she thought the baby had grown, she said he was cute, but she said "cute" the way you would about an object. She is not polite."

"Actually, Ada is shy," Oswald said.

"You think everybody is shy. And then you told me that if she came here, she would immediately call electricians and masons. Instead she called nobody; she didn't so much as move a pin. The only comment she was able to make was that this place stinks of toilets. I discovered that on my own."

"She certainly didn't say 'stinks of toilets.' She said 'stale air' or something like that."

"I can't do anything about the stink. Some buildings do smell and this one sure does. You can't imagine the money I have spent on cleaning sprays and powders. She gave me no advice about fixing this place, only told me to buy a dish rack from the five-and-ten. There's a big interior decorating idea."

"Did you buy it?"

"No. I didn't have time. I was at those damned Schlitzes' place for more than a week. They weren't mean. Actually, they were quite nice but they made me lose my milk with their meals of dried cod. Then I came here and the roof was leaking. I called a mason; I was the one who called, not your wife. Then some other disasters. I'm afraid I'm going to have to leave this apartment. My girl friend, the one who lends it to me, came with her Japanese boy friend and said she wants to set up an Oriental boutique here. I told her I didn't think this apartment was much good for that, what with the toilet stink and being on the top floor and no elevator. The Japanese was fairly nice. He said I could be the sales girl in the boutique. Anyway, boutique or not, my friend wants the apartment back because she says she needs the money. So we had a fight and split. The Japanese was still nice and promised to give me a kimono because I told him about how my coat with the dragons got burned. If she really does put me out of here, I don't know where to go. Of course, I could always go to the basement apartment. Michael won't be coming back for a while."

"The basement apartment belongs to Ada. I don't know what she intends to do with it. She may want to rent it."

"God, you all love money. I can't pay any rent now. Maybe later. That basement is dark and maybe it's damp, but its O.K. for me, and it would be nice because you are on the floor above and I could call you at night if I needed to."

"I have no intention of being wakened at night," Oswald said.

11

Dear Michael,
Your sister Angelica came to see me. I had never met her.
She is nice and very pretty. She gave me some money, sixty
thousand lire, which was a nice thought but, of course,
what's sixty thousand lire? I know you asked her to give
them to me. Thanks. I told your sister that some day I
would like to visit your mother. She says your mother is
very depressed at the moment but later, when she is not
so depressed, I can go.

Angelica gave me your address and so I can tell you I
am sorry about your father dying. Also Merry Christmas
and Happy New Year. Of course, Christmas is over. I was
alone and gloomy on Christmas day. The baby had a stuffy
nose and cried, but in the late afternoon a Japanese I know
came with a kimono. It is a black kimono with two large
sunflowers, one in front, one in back.

The good news is that I have found a job and have already begun working. In the morning I leave the baby with

a woman who looks after six others as well and in the evening I pick him up. It costs me twenty thousand lire a month. Oswald's wife, Ada, found me this job. She also found the woman who looks after the children. I think Ada is a stupid fool but I must say she has been very nice to me.

I work for a publisher named Fabio Colarosa. He is a friend of Ada's. Maybe they sleep together. Who knows? Oswald says they may have been sleeping together for two years. He is short, thin, and has a big long hooked nose. He looks like a pelican. The office is in Via Po. I am alone in a large room. Colarosa is alone in another large room. He sits at his desk and thinks. When he thinks, he wrinkles his mouth and nose. Every once in a while, he talks into the dictaphone closing his eyes and slowly caressing his hair. I am supposed to type letters and all the things he dictates to the machine.

Sometimes he simply dictates his thoughts, which are complicated, and I don't get the meaning. I am supposed to answer the telephone, but nobody ever calls him except Ada once in a while. In another big room there are two boys who pack books and design jackets. We are going to publish your aunt Matilde's book which is called something like *Polenta and Wine*. The jacket is ready. It shows the sun, and a hoe stuck in two clods of earth because it's a story about peasants. The two boys say the jacket suggests a socialist manifesto. Your mother is paying for the publication of this book. It would have been more worthwhile if she had given the money to me, who needs it. I earn fifty thousand lire a month in this job. What's fifty thousand lire? He, that's Colarosa, said he will give me a raise. He said he doesn't mind my not knowing English.

Oswald told me it took him two days to get Ada to recommend me to her friend Colarosa. She did it, but she told him that I'm nuts. He replied that he had nothing against nuts. I think that's a great answer.

At noon I go out for coffee and a sandwich. But the other day he, that's Colarosa, saw me going into the snack bar and invited me to a restaurant. He is sort of silent but not one of those who make you feel uneasy. Every once in a while he asks a very abrupt question and listens while wrinkling his mouth and nose. I had fun. I don't know why, since he talks so little, but I had fun. He explained that he wants to make a book of those thoughts he dictates to the machine. I asked him if your aunt Matilde's book was any good, and he told me it was a big mess. He is publishing it as a favor to Ada, who wants it as a favor to Oswald, who wants it as a favor to your aunt, etc., etc. Besides, your mother is paying for it.

The baby looks like you. His hair is straight and black, while yours is curly and reddish, but babies lose their hair and it grows back differently. His eyes are gray blue and yours are green, but everyone knows babies change the color of their eyes. I would like it if the baby was yours but I'm not sure. Anyway, don't think that I will ask you to be a father to him when you return. I would be stupid to ask you and I would also be a bitch since I am not sure you are the father. So this is a baby with no father, and sometimes that seems terrible, but sometimes when I'm in a good humor I think it is O.K. the way it is.

I used to have fun with you. I don't know why I had fun. It is hard to know why one person is boring and somebody else is fun. There were times when you were in a lousy mood and wouldn't talk to me. I talked and you answered, making a funny noise in your throat without opening your mouth. Now when I want to remind myself of you I make that noise in my throat and suddenly I seem to see you. The last times we were together you were always in a lousy mood. Maybe you thought I was too clinging. I didn't want anything, just to be with you. I never thought you ought to marry me, if you want to know the truth. Actually, the idea of marrying you made me laugh and also shudder.

And if I thought about it sometimes, I got rid of the idea right away.

I felt very sorry for you that time when we were supposed to meet and you rushed up terribly pale and told me that you had run over a nun. Later at your place you told me she had died. You buried your face in the pillow and I consoled you. But the next morning you wouldn't talk to me and when I stroked your hair you made that sound in your throat and pulled your head away. You have a rotten temper, but that is not the reason I don't want to marry you. I don't want to marry you because that time and many other times I felt sorry for you and I want to marry a man who never makes me feel sorry for him because I already feel so sorry for myself. I want to marry a man who makes me envy him.

So long for now and I'll write you sometimes.

Mara

12

Dear Michael,

It was marvelous to talk with you on the telephone. I could hear you perfectly. Oswald was kind enough to come and get me so I could call you from his place and he, too, could say hello to you.

I am glad to know that you go walking in the woods with all those dogs. I imagine you as you walk in the woods. I am glad I thought of sending your boots, because it must be muddy and damp. There are woods here where I could walk if I went high up on the hills and occasionally Matilde proposes that we go for a walk there, but the very thought of that Tirolean cape fluttering near me kills my desire to walk. On the other hand, I don't like the idea of going up there alone and the twins never want to come walking with me. I look at the woods from the window and they seem very remote. Maybe one must be at peace and more or less happy to walk in the woods, and I hope and trust you are both.

However, I don't understand what you plan to do. Oswald says I should leave you alone, that you are learning to speak English and to take care of a house, which in his view are both useful. Still, I would like to know when you expect to return.

I went with Oswald to get your paintings in the basement apartment. Your friend Ray lives there now, as you know. There was also a friend of Angelica's, Sonia, a girl with a black ponytail. There were others as well. A dozen people were seated on your bed and on the floor. When we entered by simply pushing open the unlocked door, they didn't move and just went on doing what they had been doing, namely nothing. Sonia helped us put the pictures in the car. The others didn't move. Once home, I hung all your paintings. I don't think they are beautiful at all, but that is just as well since you have stopped painting. Oswald says you have probably stopped for good. God only knows what you will do now. Oswald says I shouldn't think about it. You will do something.

I found it very depressing to see your apartment. I have the impression that Oswald was also depressed by the sight. The bed was unmade and I noticed the blankets that I bought for you. I don't care about them but I had told Angelica to take them for herself. It is not as if she had blankets to burn.

Matilde and I spent Christmas alone. The twins went skiing at Campo Imperatore. Angelica and Oreste were with their friends, the Bettoias, whom I do not know. Viola and Elio were with his parents in the country. Still, Matilde made a sort of Christmas dinner, although there were just the two of us to eat it in the kitchen. Cloti went to her village and we didn't think she would ever come back since she took almost all her clothes with her. Matilde made roast capon with chestnut and raisin stuffing and for dessert a Bavarian cream pudding. As a result, the kitchen was full of dirty dishes, also because the dishwasher didn't work. After dinner Matilde went to her room to nap, saying that the twins would do the dishes. She has illusions about the twins. I washed and dried the dishes. In the late afternoon Oswald appeared with his little girl Elisabeth and the dog. I gave them the leftover pudding. The little girl didn't touch it and spent her time reading the twins' magazines. Oswald fixed the dishwasher. As they were leaving, Matilde appeared and was furious that I hadn't wakened her. She said she had gone to sleep out of sheer boredom since nobody ever comes to visit us. She insisted that they stay for supper and they stayed. Thus there were still more dishes to wash since the dishwasher stopped working again and flooded the floor the instant I turned it on. The next day Cloti reappeared, contrary to our expectations. She brought us a basket of apples, and Matilde devours them, saying she should eat an apple every half hour for the sake of her health.

Oswald visits us almost every evening. According to Matilde he is in love with me, but Matilde is silly. I think he comes out of inertia, by force of habit. At first he came to listen to *Polenta and Poison* but now that is finished, thank God. Matilde would read in her deep hoarse voice as Oswald and I dozed off from exhaustion. Now Oswald has placed it with a publisher friend of Ada's. I will pay the expenses of publication because Matilde asked me to and I didn't know how to refuse.

I don't know what to make of Oswald. He is pleasant enough but he bores me. He sits around here until midnight. He leafs through magazines and rarely speaks. As a rule, he waits for me to do the talking. I make an effort but my topics of conversation with him are few. While *Polenta and Poison* was being read, we fell asleep, but at least there was an excuse for sitting there. Now I don't see any reason. And yet I must admit that when he appears I am glad.

I am used to him. When I see him come in, I feel a curious sense of relief mixed with boredom.

Fondly,

Mother

P.S. I asked Oswald if that girl Mara Pastorelli was at your place when we went to get the pictures. He said no, she is not a friend of those people. She is in another group. I sent her some money through Angelica. According to Angelica and Oswald, her situation with that poor baby was desperate. Now they have got her a job with Ada's publisher friend. Ada always copes providentially.

13

January 8, 1973

Dear Michael,
Your father's will was opened yesterday. Lillino had the will. Your father made it when he began to feel ill. I knew nothing about it. I, Lillino, Matilde, Angelica, Elio, Viola were all at the notary's office. Oreste did not come, since he had an appointment at his office.

Your father leaves you the group of paintings he did between '45 and '55, the house in Via San Sebastianello and the tower. I gather that your sisters end up with much less than you. They receive those properties near Spoleto, many of which but not all have been sold. Your father left Matilde and Cecilia his Piedmontese baroque credenza and Matilde immediately remarked that Cecilia will end up getting it because she has no use for it. You can imagine what satisfaction Cecilia, who is half blind and senile, will get from it.

You ought to let us know what you want to do about the house in Via San Sebastianello, if you want to sell or rent

75

it or go there to live. As to the tower, the architect had begun the renovations but now the work has been stopped. The plans approved by your father involve large expenditures. Lillino says that he and I should go and look at the tower and the work already done. Lillino has never seen the tower but does not think it will ever be a very sound investment because a driveway would have to be cut through the rocks in order to reach it by car. Now it is accessible only by climbing up a rocky path. I have little or no desire to climb up the rocks with Lillino.

I wish you would come and look into these matters and decide what you want. I can't decide for you. How can I, when I don't know where and how you want to live.

Mother

14

January 12, 1971

Dear Mother,

Thank you for your letters. I am writing in a hurry because I am leaving Sussex and going to Leeds with a girl I met here. This girl is supposed to teach drawing in a school in Leeds. I expect I will be able to find a job washing dishes and lighting the furnace in the same school. I have acquired great skill and speed when it comes to lighting furnaces and washing dishes.

The two people with whom I have been staying, the professor and his wife, are nice people and we separated on fairly good terms. He is a bit queer, but only a bit. He taught me to play the trumpet.

Leeds as a city can't be much. I have seen postcards of it. The girl isn't much of a girl. She is not stupid but a little boring. I am going with her because I have had enough of everything here.

Please send me some money in Leeds as soon as possible. I don't know where I will stay there, but you can send the money to me care of the girl's mother whose address is below. Also please send me Kant's *Prolegomena* to the same address and as soon as possible. You will find it in the basement apartment. I can get it here but in English and I find it difficult enough in Italian. I could probably find it in a library but I don't much like libraries. Thanks.

I can't return for the moment. Frankly, it is not that I can't but I don't want to. I don't see why you don't move into the house in Via San Sebastianello. From your letters you seem very down and bored with staying in the country.

As to the tower, decide it between you. I don't think I will ever go to live in that tower, either summer or winter.

If you don't want to move to Via San Sebastianello, maybe you could put that girl there, the one you sent the money to, Mara Castorelli. As you know she lives in Via dei Prefetti but maybe she is not comfortable there. The house in Via San Sebastianello is very comfortable. I have a happy memory of it.

Give Matilde my best wishes for her novel *Polenta and Wine*, which is about to be published. My love to the twins and everyone else.

Michael

Write me care of Mrs. Thomas, 52 Bedford Road, Leeds.

15

Dear Michael,

A very strange thing has happened to me and I can't wait to tell you about it right away. Yesterday Fabio and I made love. Fabio is the publisher Colarosa. He's the pelican. You can't imagine how much he looks like a pelican. He's Ada's friend. I took him away from Ada.

He invited me to the restaurant. Then he walked me home because it was a holiday and the office was closed in the afternoon. He said he would like to come up to see the baby. Ada had told him about the baby. I explained that the baby wasn't there. I had left him with that woman. He said he would like to see my place. I was ashamed because of the toilet stink and besides I had left everything in a mess when I went out. But I let him in because he insisted. He sat on the only chair, a torn canvas chair. I made him some Nescafé. I gave it to him in a pink plastic cup that my friend in the boardinghouse had given me. I don't have any other cups. I always meant to go and buy some in the five-and-ten but I never had time. After he drank the Nescafé he began to walk up and down wrinkling his nose. I asked him if there was a bad smell. He said no. He told me he had a big nose but didn't smell odors. I had made the bed and sat down on it. He sat next to me and then we made love. Afterward I was really amazed. He fell asleep. I watched his big sleeping nose and thought, "God, I'm in bed with a pelican."

It was five o'clock and I had to go for the baby. He woke up while I was dressing. He said he wanted to stay on for a while. I went out and returned with the baby. He was still lying there, but he raised up his nose to look at the baby and said he was a pretty baby. Then he lay back again. I fixed the baby's milk and I was glad to have him there because I don't like being alone when I fix the milk. I ought to be used to it by now because I am almost always alone but I'm not. I had a steak on hand for supper so I cooked it and we divided it. While we were eating, I told him that he looked exactly like a pelican. He said someone had already said that but he didn't remember who. "Maybe Ada," I said but I saw that he didn't much want to talk about Ada, while I did. I didn't say I thought she was dumb. I told him I thought she was a drag. He laughed. I asked him if he had had enough to eat. He said pelicans eat very little. He stayed all night. The next morning he got dressed and left. We saw each other in the office. He was sitting there with his dictaphone and winked at me when I came in but said nothing. I understood that in the office he wants to pretend nothing is going on. He didn't invite me to the restaurant. Ada came to pick him up. Now I am hungry as I have had only half a steak, two cups of coffee and a sandwich since last night. So I will go out and buy some ham.

I don't know when he will return. He didn't say. I think I am in love. He doesn't make me feel sorry for him the way you did sometimes. I envy him. I envy him because he is mysterious and dreamy. Sometimes you were dreamy but your secrets seemed childish to me while he gives the impression of having real secrets, very complicated and strange ones, which he will never tell anyone. This is why I envy him because when it comes to secrets, I don't even have half a one.

I hadn't made love for a long time, not since the baby was born, a little because I didn't happen to meet anyone, a little because I didn't like it any more. The Japanese is queer. Oswald wouldn't dream of it. Either he is queer, too, or I don't appeal to him. I don't know which.

Now Angelica is coming to get me because we are going to a friend of hers who has a baby carriage, which she keeps in the basement and doesn't need any more. Angelica says we must wash it with disinfectant.

I don't know if I'll tell Angelica about the pelican. I don't know her very well and maybe she will get the idea that I sleep with just anybody. But maybe I'll tell her because I am dying to tell someone. The minute I see Oswald I will certainly tell him. I have taken Ada's pelican away from her.

So long for now.

Mara

P.S. Angelica came. We went to get the baby carriage. It is a very good one. Along the way I told Angelica everything.

Angelica gave me your new address. She says Leeds, the city where you now are, is very gray and boring. Who knows what the hell you will do there. Angelica says you are running after a girl there. Suddenly I was jealous of this girl. You and I are friends, nothing more, and yet I am jealous of all the girls you meet.

16

Angelica got out of bed. It was Sunday. Her little girl was staying with a friend. Oreste was in Orvieto. She walked barefoot through the apartment opening the shutters. It was a sunny damp morning. The smell of pastry drifted up from the shop in the little square. She found her green sponge rubber slippers in the kitchen and put them on. Her white shower cap was on the typewriter in the dining room, and she pulled it on her head pushing all her hair under it. After her shower she put on a red terry cloth robe that was still damp because Oreste had used it the evening before. She made tea and drank it sitting in the kitchen reading yesterday's paper. She pulled off the shower cap letting her hair fall around her shoulders and went to get dressed. She searched in the drawer for a pair of tights but they all had runs. Finally she found a pair without runs but with a hole in one toe. She pulled on a pair of boots. While lacing the boots she pondered the fact that she no longer loved Oreste. She felt greatly relieved at the thought that he would be in Orvieto all day. He no longer loved her.

She thought he must be in love with the girl who edited the woman's page of the paper but then she wondered if she misjudged the situation. She put on a blue jumper dress and with a fingernail scraped a white spot on the skirt, a spot of milk and flour. Last evening she and Oreste and the Bettoias had made apple pancakes. She had rested her head on Oreste's shoulder and for a moment he had held her in his arms. Then suddenly he pushed her head away and said he was hot. He took off his coat and complained that she kept the heat on too high. The Bettoias agreed. The pancakes were rather greasy. Now in front of the mirror she gathered her hair back and looked at her long pale serious face.

The front door bell rang. It was Viola. She was wearing a new black cloth coat trimmed with leopard skin and a leopard-skin beret. Her straight glossy black hair came to her shoulders. She had a small nose and mouth and prominent white teeth. She took her coat off and carefully laid it on the trunk in the front hall. She was wearing a red blouse with a scoop neckline. Angelica poured her some tea. Viola closed her hand around the cup because she was cold. She asked Angelica why she kept the heat so low.

She had come to say that she felt the will was unfair, above all because their father had left that tower to Michael. She and Elio thought it would be marvelous if the tower went to Angelica and herself and they could use it in the summer. Michael had no use for the tower. Angelica said that she had never seen the tower but she knew that a great deal of money was needed to make it habitable and she did not have the money. Besides, the tower belonged to Michael.

"Don't be silly," Viola said. "You can get the money by selling some of the land in Spoleto." She asked for a cracker, since she had gone out without breakfast.

Angelica had no crackers but offered her some broken bread sticks in a cellophane bag. Viola began to eat the bread sticks dipped in tea. She said she thought she was pregnant because she was ten days late and felt strangely tired in the morning.

"During the first days one doesn't feel anything," Angelica said.

"Tomorrow I'll have the rabbit test," Viola said. She had calculated that the baby would be born in early August. "A terrible time to have it. I'll die of the heat. It will be awful." In two years they could all spend some time at the tower. Elio could gather mussels off the rocks. He loved gathering mussels. They would have marvelous meals of steamed mussels. They would have an outdoor barbecue and grill steaks on charcoal. Oreste and Elio could go spear fishing. Then they would grill fish instead of steak.

"Oreste has never gone spear fishing," Angelica said.

The telephone rang. Angelica went to answer it. Oswald was calling to say that Ray had been wounded in the head during a demonstration. He was at the city hospital. He asked her to come there.

Angelica put on her fake fur coat. She asked Viola to drive her to the hospital because Oreste had taken the car. On the stairs Viola said she couldn't; she didn't feel well; she was tired. Angelica said she would take a taxi. As she was getting into the taxi, Viola changed her mind and said she would drive her to the hospital. The taxi driver cursed.

In the car, Viola returned to the subject of the tower. They might build an open terrace on the top level. The baby could be put there in his carriage. The downstairs would be cool and airy.

"I don't know where you get that idea," Angelica said. "The fact is that the Isola del Giglio is hot. The sun will beat down on that terrace and roast your baby alive."

"We will put up awnings," said Viola. "And in all the rooms we might have concrete floors, which are cool, easy to clean and more durable than tiled floors."

Angelica replied that she seemed to recall that their father had selected and bought tons of tiles. Anyway, the tower belonged to Michael.

"Michael will never go there," Viola said. "He will never marry and have a family of his own. Not Michael. He's a homosexual."

"You're imagining things."

"He is a homosexual," Viola said. "Didn't you realize that he and Oswald were lovers?"

"You're imagining that," Angelica said but as she spoke she was aware that she had always thought the same thing. "Michael had a girl friend here and that girl's baby is probably his."

"He's ambidextrous," Viola said.

"Oswald has a daughter. Is he ambidextrous also?"

"Yes, ambidextrous," Viola said. "Poor Michael. My heart aches when I think of him."

"I don't think he is pathetic," Angelica said. "I feel happy when I think of him." Instead, her heart ached for him as for someone falling apart. "Michael is with a girl in Leeds now," she said.

"I know that," Viola said. "He never settles down. He drifts from place to place, tries one thing and then another. Our father ruined him. He adored and spoiled him. He took him away from us and from mother. He neglected and adored him. He always left him home alone with the old cook. That is how Michael became a homosexual. Out of loneliness. He missed Mother and us, his sisters. That's how homosexuals get that way, by thinking of women as something desired and absent. My analyst told me. As you know I go to an analyst."

"I know," Angelica said.

"I couldn't sleep. I was always tense. Since seeing the analyst I sleep better."

"Anyway Michael is not a homosexual. He is not ambidextrous. He is normal," Angelica said. "Besides, even if he were ambidextrous I don't see why we have to take the tower away from him."

Viola said she, too, would stop in at the hospital for a moment. They found Oswald, Sonia, and Ada in the waiting room of the emergency ward. Oswald had asked Ada to come because she had a doctor friend at the hospital. Sonia held Ray's windbreaker over her arm. She had been near him when they knocked him down. She knew who had done it. They were Fascists. They carried chains. Ada caught a glimpse of her doctor friend and ran after him. The doctor assured them that Ray was not seriously hurt and that he could go home.

Viola and Ada went to an espresso bar. Ada ordered coffee and Viola tonic water. Viola said she wanted to sit down for a moment because she felt faint. She was overwrought and hospitals always upset her. She had seen a nurse walk by with a basin of bloody bandages. She was afraid of having a miscarriage. Ada asked her how many months pregnant she was. One month. Ada said that in her seventh month she had stayed up for nights on end in the hospital with a maid ill with peritonitis.

Ray came out of the emergency ward with his head bandaged. Ada and Viola had left. Sonia and Angelica got in Oswald's car with Ray. They went to Oswald's place. Ray stretched out on the sofa in the living room. It was a big room with sofas and arm chairs in worn slip covers. Oswald brought in a bottle of sparkling red wine. Angelica drank a glass and curled up in an armchair with her head resting on the arm. She watched Oswald and Sonia coming and going in the kitchen. She could see Oswald's broad back in the cashmere sweater and his big head with its thin blond hair. She thought how glad she was to be there with Oswald, Sonia, and Ray and how glad she was that Viola and Ada had not come. She thought how good life was and that maybe Oswald was Michael's lover, as Viola had said, but this seemed both hard to imagine and unimportant. Ray had pulled a blanket over his head and fallen asleep. Oswald brought a tureen and placed it on the glass-topped table in front of the sofa. Sonia was bringing the soup bowls. Ray woke up and they ate spaghetti with oil, garlic, and chili. They spent the afternoon smoking, listening to records, drinking red wine and occasionally talking a little. When it was dark, Ray went back down to the basement apartment and Sonia stayed with him.

Angelica had to go home and Oswald drove her. He said he did not feel like being alone after spending such a nice afternoon doing nothing with the four of them.

Once home, Angelica watched from the window for her little girl. Oswald began to read *Ten Days That Shook the World,* which he had found on the typewriter. Angelica saw her daughter jump out of a car and wave good-bye to her friends.

The child was happy and tired. She had been to Anzio and played in the pine groves. She had had supper in a restaurant. Angelica watched her undress and helped button her pajamas. She turned off the light and kissed the blond curls. She went into the kitchen and taking a knife scraped the mud from the child's shoes onto a piece of newspaper. She put some frozen peas in boiling water and chopped some leftover ham, which she added to the peas. Oreste would return late. She sat in a chair near Oswald, pulled off her boots and considered the hole in her stocking, which had grown larger. Oswald continued to read. She put her head on the arm of the chair and fell asleep. She dreamed of the word "ambidextrous," of this single word and tiles scattered in a pine grove. The ringing of the telephone woke her. It was Elio. He begged her to come if possible. Viola was bleeding. She was in tears. Elio told Angelica she had been stupid to drag her sister to the hospital. She was upset and had had a miscarriage. Maybe it was not a miscarriage, Angelica suggested. Maybe it was just the period. Probably a miscarriage, Elio said, and Viola was in a state of despair because she wanted to have a baby so much. Angelica pulled on her boots and asked Oswald to wait until Oreste came home. She left and went to Viola.

17

Leeds, February 15, 1971

Dear Angelica,

What I write may amaze you. I am getting married. Please go to the office in San Silvestro Square and ask for the necessary documents. I don't know which ones are required. I will get married as soon as I have the documents.

I am marrying a girl I met in Leeds. Actually, she is not a girl because she is divorced with two children. She is American and teaches nuclear physics. The children are cute. I love children, not the very small ones, but the six- or seven-year-olds, like these two. I find them very amusing.

I won't go into a lot of details about the girl I am going to marry. She is thirty, not pretty, wears glasses, is very intelligent. I like intelligence.

I seem to have found a job. There is a girls' school here in Leeds that is looking for a teacher of Italian. Up to now I have been washing dishes in another school, where Josephine, the girl I came with, is teaching. You can still write me care of Josephine's mother. I don't have an apartment yet but I am looking. Eileen, the girl I am marrying, lives with her parents and the children and the house is small. There isn't room for me. I have a room in a boardinghouse but I am not giving you that address because I will move.

I may write Mother but in the meantime please begin to break the news to her. Do it gently because this sort of news upsets her. Tell her not to worry. I have thought about it carefully. Maybe we will come to Italy for the Easter vacation, and you can both meet Eileen and the children.

My best to you. Please send the documents quickly.

Michael

18

Dear Mara,

I want you to know I am getting married. The woman I am marrying is extraordinary. She is the most intelligent woman I have ever met.

Write me. Your letters amuse me. I have read them to Eileen. She is my wife, that is, she will be in about twenty days, as soon as I have received the documents. Your pelican amused us very much.

I am sending you a package with twelve little terry-cloth coveralls for the baby. Eileen wanted me to send them to you. They belonged to her children and she saved them. She says they are extremely practical, machine washable, though maybe you don't have a washing machine.

You should save them, too, so that I can have them back in case Eileen and I have children. Eileen asked me to tell you not to throw them away.

Good luck with your pelican.

Michael

19

Dear Oswald,

Forgive me for not having written you since I left. I realize that I should have written and given you detailed news about myself since we exchanged only a few words on the telephone, once when you called to tell me of my father's death and then when my mother was at your place. However, as you know I am not the letter-writing type.

I hear that you see a good deal of my family, that you spend evenings with my mother and see my sisters. I am delighted.

I am writing to tell you something that may amaze you. I have decided to get married. The name of the girl I am marrying is Eileen Robson. She is divorced with two sons. She is not pretty; in fact sometimes she is very homely. Extremely thin. Covered with freckles. She wears big glasses like Ada, but she is homelier than Ada. Maybe she is what is called a rather special type.

She is very intelligent. Her intelligence fascinates and

reassures me, perhaps because I am not intelligent but only aware and sensitive. Therefore, I can appreciate intelligence, which I lack. I write "aware and sensitive" because I remember that once you said this about me.

I could not live with a stupid woman. I am not very intelligent but I adore and revere intelligence.

In my apartment, I think, in the bottom of a bureau drawer is a scarf, a beautiful white cashmere scarf with blue stripes. My father gave it to me as a present. I wish you would get it and wear it. I would like to think of you with that scarf around your neck when you leave your shop and walk along the Tiber. I have not forgotten our long walks back and forth along the Tiber at sunset.

Michael

20

February 22, 1971

Dear Michael,

The cashmere scarf has disappeared. However, I have bought myself a scarf; I don't think it is cashmere and it has no blue stripes. A simple white scarf. I wear it and imagine that it is yours. I realize it is a substitute, but all our lives are made up of substitutes.

I often visit your mother, who is very nice and, as has been reported to you, I see members of your family frequently.

Otherwise, my life is the same as ever, just as when you were here. I go to the shop, listen to Mrs. Schlitz complain about her varicose veins and arthritis; I leaf through the accounts, talk with occasional customers, take Elisabeth to her gym class and go to pick her up; I walk along the Tiber, and with my hands in my pockets stand leaning over the bridge watching the sun set.

I send you my best wishes for your marriage and have sent you a present of *Les Fleurs du mal*, bound in red Morocco.

Oswald

21

Dear Michael,

Angelica is here and tells me that you are getting married. She says you told her to break the news gradually in order not to upset me. Instead, she told me the news instantly, the moment she came into the room. Angelica knows me better than you do. She knows that I am so continuously upset that nothing upsets me any more. You may find it strange, but since I am in a continuous state of fright and disbelief, there's nothing that can amaze or frighten me.

I didn't write you because I have been sick in bed for ten days. I called Dr. Bovo, your father's doctor who lives on the fourth floor in Via San Sebastianello. I have pleurisy. I find it extremely odd to write "I have pleurisy" because I have never had anything wrong in my life and have always thought of myself as very healthy. It's the other people who always got sick.

Angelica gave me your letter to read. Several sentences in it amazed me, although I am, as I said, beyond that. "I like intelligence. I love children." Frankly, I was unaware that you were so enchanted with intelligence and children. However, I get the impression that finally you are trying to be clearheaded and decisive, that finally, you are trying to make a definite choice.

I will be glad to see you at Easter and to meet your wife and her children. The very thought of having children in the house exhausts me but since I will see you, I will welcome everyone gladly.

This woman you are marrying is thirty years old, but I don't regard that as a disadvantage. Obviously, you need a woman older than yourself at your side. You need maternal affection because your father took you away from me when you were little. May God forgive him, assuming God exists, which is not beyond the realm of possibility. Sometimes I think about how little we have been together, you and I, and how little we know each other, how superficially we evaluate each other. I think you are very scatterbrained but I don't really know whether you are scatterbrained or sensible in your own curious way.

It seems that at long last I will get a telephone. Thanks to Ada, who went personally to the telephone company as soon as she heard I was sick.

I have forgotten something important. Oswald says that Ada would be glad to buy your tower. You would be smart to sell it and thus get out of a mess, although I realize that you never even think about the tower. Viola and Elio wanted to buy it from you but they were very disappointed once they saw it. They say there is a long hot climb up a steep path to get to it. Furthermore, this tower looks as if it would collapse at the slightest touch. That architect has not done any work as yet, except to have a couple of masons take out a sink and knock down a wall. The tiles have been selected and purchased but they are still stored at the factory, which is beginning to complain. Ada says that the architect is a real idiot. She showed the tower to her architect. She wants to put in a swimming pool and to build a stairway down to the sea and a driveway. Now it turns out that your father paid ten million lire for this tower, not one million, as he claimed. Ada will give you fifteen. You ought to make up your mind.

I guess you will need shirts and socks and perhaps a dark suit. I can't do anything about it now since I am sick and Angelica doesn't have time. Viola's morale is low, she is depressed, she has had a slight nervous breakdown. We are all in bad shape. Matilde has lost her head completely over *Polenta and Poison*. She goes every day to the publisher Colarosa to read proof, look at the book jacket, and to pester him. Your friend Mara Martorelli works for Colarosa now. Matilde saw her there and says she was wearing an unbelievable Japanese kimono with enormous flowers.

I am stopping because Angelica is waiting to mail this letter.

With my love and wishes for much happiness, assuming that there is such a thing as happiness, something that may be possible even if we rarely see traces of it in the world that is given to us.

Mother

22

February 29, 1971

Dear Michael,

I have received the twelve terry-cloth overalls. You could have skipped sending them because several are worn out, the fasteners don't work and, besides, they are all as stiff and hard as dried cod. Tell your Eileen or whatever her name is that I am not a beggar. And tell her that my baby has lovely new soft coveralls of a charming pink-and-blue-flowered terry cloth. All the same I send my thanks.

I am writing to announce that I have moved in with the pelican. I arrived here two nights ago with all my stuff because my girl friend told me to get out of Via dei Prefetti. I told her about the pelican and so she said I didn't need Via dei Prefetti any more and that I should clear out right away. She is thinking of turning the apartment into a sort of club, or a gallery, or something like that. The boutique is out. Anyway, she said she needed money, lots of money and I ought to get out without a fuss. I certainly could have stuck it out and stayed on but instead I got mad. In twenty minutes I packed all my stuff, took the baby and piled everything in the carriage and came to Fabio's. The pelican has a penthouse on Campitelli Square. It is a marvelous penthouse, a real change from that place in Via dei Prefetti. He was rather frightened by my arrival in the evening but he immediately sent the housekeeper out to get milk for the baby and a chicken for me from the Pigeon, the rotisserie in Largo Argentina. I don't know if I told you that the baby now drinks whole milk. No more powdered milk.

I had been to Fabio's place before and I liked the penthouse very much. The only thing I don't like is his housekeeper, a big tough fiftyish woman who is not at all nice. She looks at me sternly and doesn't answer when I speak to her. She looks at the baby as if he was a poor weak little thing. I told Fabio he ought to fire her. He shilly-shallies and says she is a good housekeeper.

I don't go to the office any more. I stay here, enjoy this penthouse, and sun on the terrace. I put the baby on the terrace under an umbrella and you can't imagine how great it is to be here. I don't take the baby to that woman any more because she neglected him, didn't change him, and I am sure she left him to cry. When Fabio comes back from the office, he sits on the terrace, we hold hands, and have Belinda, that's the fiftyish old housekeeper in a red apron, bring us tomato juice. In the beginning Fabio was a bit frightened but now when I ask him if he is happy, he wrinkles his big nose and says yes. He has got rid of Ada. He doesn't see her any more. I telephoned Oswald to find out how Ada took it. He said she took it badly but predicted that our relationship won't last long. I think that I will marry the pelican. I will have some more babies because the thing I like best is to have babies. Of course, to have babies one must have money; otherwise it is awful, but he, the pelican, is a millionaire I am sure. It is not that I am marrying him for his money; I am marrying him because I love him. However, I am glad he has all this money; I envy him because he is rich and intelligent and sometimes I find myself envying him that enormous nose.

I send you lots of congratulations for your marriage. Send me yours for mine because you will see that I will be married almost before you.

As a wedding present I am giving you a painting by Mafai. I will not ship it because it is not a simple matter to ship a painting by Mafai. It hangs here at the pelican's in our bedroom and I asked the pelican if I could make you a present of it and he said yes.

Mara

23

Leeds, March 18, 1971

Dear Angelica,

I received the documents. Many thanks. I got married on Wednesday.

I hear that Mother is sick and I am sorry. I hope it is nothing serious.

Eileen and I found a little two-storied house on Nelson Road, a big road that passes through a vast section of identical little houses. I plan to grow roses in our garden, which measures about six and a half feet.

Thank Mother for the money, shirts, and the dark suit, which I didn't wear at my wedding and won't ever wear. I have hung it in a closet with moth balls.

Eileen goes to the university early in the morning and drops the children off at school. I go out a little later. I straighten up the house, rinse the breakfast dishes and run the vacuum over the carpets. All of this has been going on, however, only for the past two days. Anyway, everything is all right.

On my wedding day we gave a dinner at a restaurant with Eileen's parents. They adore me.

I learned that Viola and Elio wanted to come to the wedding. That relative of Mrs. Schlitz's told me, the one who appeared at the boardinghouse where I was living until the day before yesterday. Fortunately, they did not come. Fortunately, none of you came. It's not that I don't want to see you. I would be glad to see all of you, but we got married in a great hurry and skipped the usual formalities so that Viola and Elio and you, too, if you had come, might have been disappointed.

Tell Oreste that my wife is a member of the Communist Party, one of the very few Communists here. I am still non-Communist. I am still nothing and I am out of touch with those friends I had in Rome and have no news from them. To think that I left for political reasons, not entirely for those reasons but partially. Well, I can't really figure out why I left. Anyway, I don't bother about politics; my wife does that and it is enough for me.

Would you send me a book, *The Critique of Pure Reason* by Kant? See if you can find it in my basement, assuming that the apartment is still there and I can still call it mine.

My best to you.

Michael

24

March 23, 1971

Dear Michael,

For two days I have been up and about and I am fine. I still feel a little weak but that will pass.

I would welcome a letter from you, but you are stingy about writing your mother. Angelica gave me your news. I am glad you have a charming house, at least I envisage it as charming, with that little garden and the carpets. I can't see you running the vacuum over the carpets. I can't see you growing roses. I can't think about roses right now. I have the feeling that I wouldn't know how to grow them and yet I came to live in the country for this purpose. Maybe I feel the way I do because it is still winter and quite cold and it rains a lot but I suspect that even come spring I won't bother about the garden. I will probably call in a gardener and I won't touch a leaf. I don't have a green thumb as Ada has, from what everyone says. Besides, roses remind me of the house in Via dei Villini where I had a beautiful rosebush under my window. It grew in the neighboring garden, not in ours. In fact, roses remind me of Philip. Not that I don't want to remember him. I think of him thousands of times and am linked to him by innumerable strands of memory but I must have been looking at the roses while he was saying that it was all over between us and now whenever I see a rose bush I feel as if I were going to black out. So there may be flowers in my garden but there won't be any roses.

Since you and I are alike in many ways, I doubt that you are cut out to be a flower grower. Still it is possible that you have changed during these months and become a different person from the one I knew. And Eileen may turn you into still another person. I have faith in Eileen. I think I will like her. I wish you would send me her photograph. The one you sent is so small that all I can see is a long raincoat. You say she is very intelligent. I, too, like intelligence. I have always tried to be with intelligent people. Your father was a strange and talented man. We could not live together, perhaps because our characters were too strong and both of us needed a lot of leeway. Philip is strange and very intelligent. Unfortunately he has cut himself off from me. He has gone out of my life entirely. We don't see each other any more. We could have remained friends if I had wanted it that way but I didn't. Anyway, we would have had to see each other in the presence of that bony-faced female he married. She must be utterly stupid. Maybe he found our relationship a strain. I don't consider myself very intelligent but maybe I was too intelligent for him. Not everyone admires intelligence. I have lovely memories of those years with Philip, even if it all fell apart the way it did and ended in darkness and emptiness. He never wanted to come and live with me and made all sorts of excuses: the twins would disturb his studying, or the problem was his health or his mother's health. But they were all excuses. Actually, he really didn't want to live with me. Maybe he didn't love me enough. Still I have a happy memory of those hours he spent at our house in Via dei Villini. He played chess with Viola and Angelica, helped the twins with their homework, made curried rice, typed his book in my room, a book he later published as *Religion and Pain*. I thought a lot about Philip while I was sick and I even wrote him a letter but I tore it up. A few days ago they had a baby girl. They sent me a card with a red stork on it. Idiots. They have named the child Vanessa. Idiots. What sort of a name is that to hang on a little girl.

As I write I am sitting near the fire in my room. From the window I can see our flat empty garden with two fake wrought-iron carriage lamps that I bought without thinking, and Matilde's two miniature firs, which I loathe. I can see the town in the distance and the hills with the moon. I am wearing a black dress that I think is becoming and when I go down to dinner I will throw over my shoulders the Spanish shawl your father gave me some twenty years ago; I dug it out of a cedar chest. Oswald and Colarosa, the publisher, are coming to dinner. Matilde invited Colarosa. He deserved the invitation because Matilde has pestered him to death. *Polenta and Poison* has finally been published. The house is crawling with copies of *Polenta and Poison*. Matilde sent you a copy with her dedication. So you, too, will see the clods, the sun, and the hoe. Matilde designed the jacket. Colarosa suggested a reproduction of a painting by Van Gogh but he got nowhere. When Matilde gets an idea, you can't budge her. Everyone told her that her design looks like a pronouncement of the Socialist Party. There was no way to change her mind.

Yesterday Matilde went to Rome to buy champagne for this evening. She planned the dinner and today she has been in the kitchen the entire day, driving Cloti, who was already nervous and ill-tempered, out of her mind. There will be sartù of rice, *vol-au-vent* with chicken and béchamel sauce, and meringues. I pointed out to Matilde that every course was circular in shape and, in addition, very rich. A meal like that could kill an ox.

Matilde wants the twins to get rid of their ponytails and wear their hair down and to put on their velvet dresses with the lace collars for this evening. She is going to wear the skirt to her black suit and a cossack overblouse. I haven't met Colarosa as yet. Matilde says he is short, with his head embedded in his shoulders and a nose beyond description. I wanted Ada to come but Oswald explained that Ada and Colarosa had been lovers and have split up. Now he has taken up your friend Mara Castorelli, who descended on him at home late one evening with her baby. To think that it was Ada who recommended Mara to him and Mara immediately took him away from her. I do not know if Mara is coming tonight. I said it was all right with me, but she may not be able to leave the baby. However, I will invite Ada another time. I have not met her, but even so she has been incredibly nice to me. Thanks to her I will get a telephone. I can't believe it and I will call you immediately. Still the thought of telephoning you upsets me. I guess my nerves and heart are not as good as they used to be. To think I was strong as a horse once. I have been through too much. I am frail now.

There is the sound of a car. They have arrived. I must leave you.

Mother

I saw a small person in a mink coat get out of the car. It must be Mara.

25

Dear Michael,

A few evenings ago, I was at your mother's for dinner. It was not much fun. Oswald, Angelica, the pelican, your aunt, your mother and your little sisters were there. Some time ago I terribly wanted to meet your mother and wanted her to like me, but now I can't imagine why. Maybe I hoped she would help me marry you. I never really wanted to marry you. That's for sure. At least, I never thought I wanted to but maybe out of desperation I did want to unconsciously.

That night at your mother's I wore a long black and silver skirt bought that afternoon for the occasion with the pelican, and my mink coat also bought with the pelican five days ago. I kept the fur coat around my shoulders because your mother's house is icy cold. The radiators don't work properly. It's difficult to explain, but at first I felt very tender and tiny in that skirt and fur coat. I wanted everybody to look at me and to see how tender and tiny I was. I wanted this so much that when I spoke, my voice came out thin and sweet. Then at a certain point I thought, "Maybe these people think that I am a 'tart of the upper echelon.'" I had read the phrase "tart of the upper echelon" in a mystery story that morning. The minute I thought of this I felt completely let down. Then I was sure everyone was treating me very coldly. Oswald, too, and Angelica and also the pelican. He had sunk down into an armchair with a glass in his hand. He stroked his hair. He stroked his nose. He didn't wrinkle it; he just stroked it very slowly. Your mother is beautiful but I am not sure I like her. She wore a black dress and a shawl with a fringe. She toyed with the fringe and with her hair, which is curly and reddish and exactly like yours. I thought that if you had been in that room, it would have made everything easier for me because you know very well that I am not a tart of upper or lower echelon. You know I am just a girl and that's all. There was a fire in the fireplace, but I was cold just the same.

Your mother asked where I was from and I said Novi Ligure. Then I began to tell a few lies about Novi Ligure. I said I had a lovely big house there with lots of cousins who looked forward to my coming and that I have a dear old nurse there and a little brother whom I adore. In fact, the nurse is an old woman who comes in to cook for my cousins. I am fond of my little brother but I never write to him. And that house of my cousins is nothing special. It is over a china shop. My cousins sell china. I didn't say so. I said my cousins were all lawyers.

Your mother and Angelica were busy in the kitchen because your mother's housekeeper got sick all of a sudden and went to bed. Actually, she was annoyed with your aunt over some comment about the pastry shells. Angelica told me this. Your little sisters refused to help, saying they were too tired. They had been playing volleyball. They had on their gym clothes and didn't want to change and your aunt was mad about that, as well as about the pastry shells which were all soft and mushy inside.

At a certain point I felt terribly depressed. I thought, "What am I doing here? Where am I? What kind of a fur coat have I got on? What sort of people are these who barely speak to me and when I talk act as if they didn't hear?" I told your mother I would like to show her the baby. She told me to bring him but she said it without any enthusiasm. I was dying to yell that the baby was yours. If I had been one hundred per cent sure, I would have shouted it. I saw photographs of you when you were little and I picked them up and noticed that the baby has your chin and mouth. But I can't be sure. Such likenesses are always so questionable.

They talked very little but I didn't understand a word they said. They are intellectuals. I was dying to yell that they were all shitheads. I didn't even like Angelica any more. I didn't understand anybody. The pelican was terribly serious. He didn't look at me. Every once in a while I caressed his hand. He pulled it away. He seemed to be on pins and needles when I talked. He had never seen me with other people and maybe he was ashamed of me. At the end of meal they poured the champagne. I said, "All the best to *Polenta and Chestnuts.*" I got the title wrong. The pelican corrected me. I explained that I got mixed up because of the song that goes, "Don't go up in the mountains. You will eat polenta and chestnuts. You will get acid indigestion." I sang the entire song. It's a cute song and I can carry a tune. Your mother smiled a little. Oswald smiled a little. The pelican didn't smile at all. The twins didn't smile at all. As I was singing I realized that I was being given the big freeze. Your aunt kept going to knock on the housekeeper's door to offer her some pastry shells and other dishes and came back crushed because the housekeeper refused it all.

Angelica, the pelican, and I went home in Oswald's car.

109

I was in the back seat with the pelican. I said, "I don't know what you have against me. What did I do to you? You didn't say a word to me, never looked at me all evening." He said, "I have a bad headache." "Christ, you always have a headache," I told him. It is true, he does always have a headache. He sat all crunched in the back of the car as if it bothered him even to touch me. Then I began to cry, not out loud, but quietly and the tears fell on the fur coat. Angelica patted me on the knee. Oswald was driving and didn't look back. The pelican hid in his corner with his overcoat pulled around him. His nose was motionless. It was awful to be crying in that freezing atmosphere, worse than to be singing. Much worse.

I had left the baby at home with Belinda, the housekeeper. I should have taken him with me. Belinda has no patience with children. I found the baby screaming. Belinda was still up and said she had a right to some sleep. I said I had a right to enjoy myself a little and to some sleep. She answered that I didn't have a right to anything. I didn't reply just then. I slammed the door in her face and then yelled that she was fired. But I have already fired her lots of times. She says she won't leave, that the doctor has to fire her. The doctor is the pelican. The baby cried all night. It was awful. He is teething, poor thing. I walked back and forth with him in the living room and all the while I was crying. Toward morning he fell asleep and I put him in his carriage. I felt sorry for him because he was exhausted and sweaty from crying, his hair sticky and wet, and he lay limp as a rag. I felt sorry for myself, too, because I was dead tired and still in my black and silver evening skirt. I went into the bedroom. The pelican was awake, lying with his head cradled in his hands. I felt terribly sorry for him and everything about him, his pajamas, his head on the pillow, his nose. I said to him, "Don't think I want to go on this way. We have got to get a nurse for the baby." "A nurse?" he said flabbergasted. I told him, "When I was in Via dei Prefetti alone, I could let the baby cry a little and it didn't matter but I can't have him crying here because you always have a headache." "I don't think I want a nurse here in addition to everything else," he said. "No, I don't think I want anything of the sort." "Well, then, I will go back to living alone." I said. He didn't reply. So we lay there as still and cold as two corpses.

In a previous letter I wrote you that the pelican and I would get married. That was stupid. Pretend that I never said it. Tear up the letter because I am ashamed of having written it. He never dreamed of marrying me and maybe I don't want to marry him.

Now he has gone. Before he went out, I yelled, "And don't treat me like a tart of the upper echelon." My voice was no longer soft the way it sounded when I felt tender and tiny. Suddenly my voice was as loud and harsh as a fish wife's. He said nothing. He left.

Sometimes I feel furious. I say to myself, "Here I am, cute, pretty, young, nice, and I have such a pretty baby. I do him the favor of staying in his house and spending his money which is of no use to him. After all, what does he want, the broken-assed bastard." Sometimes I am furious and that is what I think.

Mara

26

Novi, March 29, 1971

Dear Angelica,

I am writing you from Novi Ligure, which may come as a surprise. I got here yesterday. The baby and I are staying with a woman who works in my cousins' house. She is old. Her name is Amelia. She said I could stay for a few days, but no more, because there isn't room. I don't know where to go but it doesn't matter because I always manage somehow.

I left unexpectedly. I left a note for Fabio. He was not home. I wrote, "I am going. Thanks. Good-bye." I took the mink coat with me because he had given it to me as a present and anyway I was cold. I also took the black and silver skirt, the one I wore at your mother's. It was of no use to him. Anyway, the coat and skirt were presents.

I have to ask you for a favor. In the rush of leaving I forgot my kimono, the black one with the sunflowers. Please get it and send it to me here Via della Genovina 6, Novi Ligure. It must be in our room in the bottom drawer of the bureau. I see I have written "our room." For a while he and I were happy in that room. If there is such a thing as happiness that was it. The only trouble is that it lasted such a short time. I guess happiness doesn't last long. Everyone has always said it doesn't last.

You probably think me weird to fall in love with a man like that, not at all good-looking with that big nose. A pelican. When I was a child I had a book with pictures of all the animals and there was one of a pelican standing with his feet planted firmly on the ground and with an enormous pink beak. My pelican exactly. Well, I have learned that one can fall in love with anybody, even if he is comical, strange, sad. I liked his having a lot of money because his money seemed different from other people's. It seemed to trail behind him like the tail of a comet. I liked his being so intelligent, his knowing a lot of things that I don't know, and his intelligence seemed like a long tail. I don't have a tail. I am stupid and poor.

When I first met the pelican, I had some nasty ideas. I was not at all sentimental. I thought, "I am going to rip this guy off, spend his money. I'm going to get him away from that stupid Ada, set myself up with the baby in his house and nobody will get me out." I was cold, calm, and happy. Then, little by little, I felt this depression inside me. I caught it from him, the way you catch a disease. I felt it in my bones, even when I slept, and I couldn't get rid of it. As he got more depressed, he became much more intelligent. I just became stupider. Depression affects everyone differently.

Then I realized I had fallen into a trap. I was madly in love with him and he didn't give a damn about me. He was fed up having me underfoot. He didn't have the guts to throw me out because he felt sorry for me. And I felt sorry for him. It was exhausting to live in the midst of all that pity, exhausting for both of us.

I don't think he ever gave a damn about Ada but she was strong, optimistic, active, and not at all clinging. I was clinging and a drag. There he was lost in his gloom and depression and I understood that there was no place for me in those feelings of his. I would never be part of them and this "never" was frightening. So I left.

When I arrived at Amelia's last night, she was scared. For three years she had not heard from me or seen me. I have never even sent her a postcard. She didn't know that I had had a baby. She looked at the baby and the fur coat and couldn't make sense out of it. I told her I had had a baby by a man who then dumped me. I asked her to give me a place to sleep. She pulled a mattress out of a closet. I told her I was hungry and she gave me a fried egg and a dish of beans for supper. I knew she was letting me stay there because she felt sorry for me. Life seems to be a matter of everybody making everybody feel sorry for everybody.

Amelia goes to cook for my cousins every day. There are lots of them and lots of cooking to do. I told her not to say anything about me to my cousins but she told them first thing that I had returned and was at her place. As a result, two of my cousins and my brother came. My brother, who is twelve years old, lives with my cousins and helps in their store. I am very fond of him but he was not at all affectionate. He was cold, not at all surprised about the baby. He made no fuss over him and my cousins didn't either. If I had held a cat in my arms, they would have made more of a fuss. Instead, my cousins were interested in the fur coat that they saw on a chair. They said I could get along for years on what I could get for it. I knew they were figuring on buying it from me. I said I had no intention of selling it now. I am fond of my fur coat. I remember the day when we went out to buy it, the pelican and I, hand in hand. Then he still seemed happy to go walking with me. Maybe he was already beginning to think that I was clinging and a drag but I didn't realize it.

If the pelican asks for my address you can give it to him.

Regards,

Mara

27

Dear Mara,

Angelica came to get your kimono. It took us a long time to find it because it wasn't in the drawer in the bedroom. It turned up in my study under a pile of newspapers. It was dusty and I didn't know whether or not to ask Belinda to wash it, but then I didn't want to remind Belinda of you. The morning after you left she destroyed every trace of you. She threw out all the cosmetics you left in the bathroom and all the jars of baby food. I said I liked baby food but she said these were an inferior brand. Angelica shook and brushed your kimono and said she would mail it to you the way it was.

I am sending you some money because I expect you will need it. Angelica has just gone to the post office to mail your kimono and to wire you the money.

I am deeply grateful to you for leaving. I was longing for you to leave, which you understood, and of course my behavior was such that you could hardly miss the point.

116

These words may strike you as unnecessarily cruel. Indeed, they are cruel but not unnecessary. If deep down you have any thought of returning, forget it. I cannot live with you. I cannot live with anyone probably. I made the mistake of deceiving both myself and you that a lasting relationship was possible between us. However, I didn't ask you to come in the first place. You came on your own. Our relationship, which was tenuous to begin with, fell apart as soon as we started living together. I know I made mistakes and I don't want to minimize my guilt toward you. Those mistakes have added to the burden of guilt I bear toward life, a considerable burden as it is. I felt great pity for you and I couldn't bring myself to tell you to get out. You will think me a coward. The word fits me precisely. I feel sorry for you and for myself with the gloomy pity of a coward and when I came home the other evening and didn't find you but found your note I missed you and sat down in my chair with a feeling of emptiness. However, I also felt a great sense of relief and joy, and it is only right that you should know this. In short, I could not stand you anymore.

I wish you the very best and I hope you are happy, assuming there is such a thing as happiness, which I doubt. But others believe in happiness, and who is to say that they are not right.

The Pelican

28

Dear Angelica,

Mara has written me. Go to see her and cheer her up. She has lots of problems. That publisher she was living with, besides having committed the crime of publishing *Polenta and Poison* has infected her with all sorts of complexes and depressions.

I may come for Easter vacation but I am not sure. Sometimes I miss all of you, namely "one's own people," so called, even if you are not mine, as I am not yours. However, if I should come, you would watch me; I would feel all of you watching me. And since my wife would be with me, you would scrutinize her as well and try to figure out what sort of relationship she and I have. I couldn't bear this.

I also miss my friends Gianni, Anselmo, Oliviero, and all the others. I have no friends here. And I miss certain sections of Rome. Then I both miss and am revolted by the thought of other friends and other parts of the city. This mixture of affection and loathing makes the places and people I love seem very remote and the means to reach them inadequate and impractical.

At times my homesickness and revulsion are so intertwined and intense that I feel them in my sleep and I wake up and have to get out of bed and smoke a cigarette. Eileen takes her pillow and goes to sleep in the children's room. She says she has a right to her sleep. She says everyone has to cope with his own nightmares by himself. She is right. She certainly isn't wrong about that.

I don't know why I am writing all these things to you. It is one of those times when I would talk to an empty chair. I can't talk to Eileen, first, because it is Saturday and she is in the kitchen preparing meals for the entire week and second, because she doesn't like to sit and listen to people talk. Eileen is very intelligent, but I have discovered that her intelligence is no good to me because it is directed toward things that don't concern me such as nuclear physics. Really I would prefer a stupid wife who would listen to me patiently and stupidly. Right now I wouldn't mind having Mara here. I couldn't stand her for long because after she had listened to me, she would dump all her problems in my lap and she would stick to me like toffee and never leave me in peace. Certainly I would not want her for a wife. However, right now I wouldn't mind having her here.

My best to you.

Michael

29

April 2, 1971

Dear Michael,

I have just received your letter and am terribly distressed by it. Obviously you are very unhappy.

Perhaps I should not take your letter too literally. Perhaps you have merely had a fight with your wife and are feeling lonely, but I can't convince myself of this. I am frightened.

I might be able to come and visit you if you don't come here. I cannot easily leave my little girl and Oreste and I don't have the money for the trip but that is the least of the problems because I could ask Mother for it. She isn't very well; she runs a temperature every now and then. Obviously I won't tell her that I have received a frightening letter from you. If I do decide to leave and to ask her for the money, I will tell her that you can't leave your work and so I thought I'd pay you a visit.

You say that at this moment you don't want to have to meet the eyes of the people who love you. Indeed it is hard to tolerate the eyes of people who love us at such a time, but that difficulty can be overcome quickly. The eyes of people who love us can be extremely clear, merciful, and severe in their judgments. It can be hard to confront them but in the end it can be good and helpful for all of us to face clarity, severity, and mercy.

Your friend Mara has left Colarosa. She wrote to me. She is in Novi Ligure, living in the house of a woman who works for her cousins. She is in a bad way with no place to live and nothing in the world but a kimono with sunflowers, a mink coat, and a baby. I have the feeling that all of us in some subtle way manage to create hopeless situations for ourselves in which there are no solutions and from which there are no exits.

Drop me a line saying if it is all right for me to come. I don't want to come if you can't bear the thought of seeing me.

Angelica.

30

Leeds, April 5, 1971

Dear Angelica,

Don't come. We are expecting some of Eileen's relatives from Boston and have only one guest room. Then we may all go to Bruges. I don't know Bruges.

I have never met these relatives of Eileen. There are times when it is good to be with strangers.

Don't try to read between the lines. Anyway, all your conjectures would be mistaken because you lack the essential facts.

I would have been happy to see you, but we can meet some other time.

Michael

31

Dear Michael,

Your letter just came. My bag was already packed. I got the money from Oswald, not from Mother. For once he had the cash without having to look to Ada for help.

That phrase in your letter, "I don't know Bruges, "made me laugh, as if Bruges was the only thing in the world you don't know.

I wanted to see you not only to talk about you but also about myself. I, too, am going through a difficult period.

But, as you say, another time.

                                        Angelica

32

April 9, 1971

Dear Michael,

Angelica tells me you won't be coming for Easter vacation. Never mind. By now I have said "never mind" countless times while thinking of you. It is true that one grows more patient as the years pass. That is the only thing that grows. All one's other faculties tend to deteriorate.

I had fixed up the two rooms on the top floor, made the beds, and hung towels in the bathroom that is the prettiest bathroom in the house. It has green tiles set in arabesques and as I looked at it I felt happy at the thought that your wife would see it. The rooms are still ready with the beds made. I haven't been up there since. Now I will tell Cloti to go and strip the beds.

While I was preparing those two rooms, I was thinking that your wife would feel at home and that she would see what a good housekeeper I am. However, such thoughts were stupid because I don't know your wife or when and where she feels at home and I don't know if she is one of those people who likes both a well-run house and the person who runs it well.

Angelica told me you are going to Bruges instead. I am not going to ask what you are going to do in Bruges because by now I have given up asking what you are up to anywhere. I try to visualize your life in one place or another but at the same time I realize that your life does not correspond to my notion of it and so I grow more and more disheartened and my imagination falters attempting to weave its arabesques around you.

When my health is better I would like to come with Angelica for a visit if you like the idea. We won't stay at your house because I don't want to bother your wife, who must be very busy. We will stay at a hotel. I don't like to travel and I dislike hotels. However, I prefer hotels to the feeling that I am taking up space in a small house and being a bother. One of the few things I know about your life is that you have a small house. I can't leave now because I have not yet recovered from that pleurisy, that is, I am over the pleurisy, but the doctor says I must be careful. He has discovered that there is something wrong with my heart. Explain to your wife that I am a person whose house is neat and tidy and whose heart is a mess. Describe me to her so that when she meets me she can compare the real me with your descriptions. One of the rare pleasures in life is to compare the descriptions of others with our fantasies and then with the reality.

I think of your wife often and I try to visualize her, even if you didn't bother to describe her and that photograph you sent when you wrote that you were getting married is small and blurred. I look at it often but all I can make out is a long black raincoat and a head wrapped in a scarf.

You never write to me but I am glad you write Angelica. I guess it is natural for you to write her because you are closer to her than to me. Maybe I delude myself but I think that in communicating with her you are secretly communicating with me as well. Angelica is very intelligent. I think she is the most intelligent of you all although it is hard to judge the intelligence of one's children.

Sometimes I have the feeling that she is not happy. Angelica tells me very little, not out of a lack of affection but because she doesn't want to worry me. It is strange but Angelica takes a maternal attitude toward me. When I question her about herself, her replies are always marked by a cold calm. In the end, I know very little about Angelica. When we are together, we don't talk about her but about me. I am always glad to talk about myself because I am so much alone but since I am alone there isn't very much to tell about myself. What I mean is that I haven't much to say about how I spend my time. Now that I am unwell my days are more monotonous than ever. I go out very little, rarely take the car. I sit for hours in a chair and watch Matilde doing her yoga, Matilde playing solitaire, Matilde typing a new book, Matilde making a beret from scraps of wool.

Viola told me she is angry with you because you haven't written her so much as a postcard. She bought you a lovely silver tray as a wedding present and planned to give it to you when you came. Do write to Viola and thank her, because the tray is very handsome. Also write to the twins, who were looking forward to your visit. They had bought presents for Eileen's children, namely a switchblade and a tent for playing cowboys and Indians. And, of course, do write to me.

Yesterday Oswald left for Umbria with Elisabeth and Ada. So for a week we will be without his evening visits. I got used to seeing him appear here in the evenings. I got used to having him around with his big square head, his thin carefully groomed hair, and his ruddy face.

He, too, must have grown accustomed to spending his evenings in this house playing Ping-Pong with the twins and reading Proust out loud to Matilde and me. When he doesn't come here, he goes to Angelica and Oreste where he does more or less the same things with the slight difference that he reads Mickey Mouse to the little girl and plays bingo with Oreste and the Bettoias. Oreste thinks him pleasant but aimless. The Bettoias think him aimless but nice. Actually one cannot dislike him. I don't think he can be called aimless because one expects nothing from an aimless person, whereas one expects that Oswald will suddenly open up and reveal his motives for living. I think he is very intelligent, but he keeps his intelligence well guarded somewhere behind his smiling face and his broad chest. For some unknown reason he doesn't use his intelligence. He strikes me as very sad in spite of his smile. Maybe I got used to his companionship because I like sadness. I like sadness more than I like intelligence.

You and Oswald were friends, and I have rarely had the pleasure of knowing one of your friends. At times I ask him about you, but he replies with the same cold calm that Angelica displays when I ask her if everything is all right and if she is happy. I am under the impression that Oswald, too, wants to avoid worrying me. Afterward, when I think back on his calm voice and his quiet evasive replies, I loathe him, but when he is here I keep quiet and accept his silences and vague answers. Over the years I have become meek and resigned.

The other day I remembered the time when you came here and immediately began rummaging in all the closets for a Sardinian rug you wanted to hang on the wall in your apartment. That must have been the last time I saw you. I had just moved into this house. It was in November. You wandered from room to room, rummaging in the closets where things had just been unpacked and put away, and I followed you complaining that you were always making off with my things. You must have found and taken that Sardinian rug with you because it isn't here and it wasn't in the basement apartment either. Actually I didn't care about the rug then and don't care now. I remember it now because it is connected with the last time I saw you. I remember that while I was getting angry and complaining I felt very happy. I knew that my complaints would make you feel both happy and irritated. Now I think of that day as a happy time. Unfortunately we rarely recognize moments of happiness while we are living them. Usually we recognize them in the perspective of the past. My happiness was to complain, yours to rummage in my closets. Still, I must admit that we let a precious moment slip away from us that day. We could have sat down together and talked about essentials. Probably we would have been less happy, or even been unhappy. However, now I could look back on that day not just as a vague sort of happy time but as a crucial moment in which you and I spoke truthfully and really communicated in clear and essential terms as persons instead of as people who have only talked around each other with gray, good-natured, and useless words.

Fondly,

Mother

33

Leeds, April 30, 1971

Dear Angelica,

I am a friend of Eileen and Michael. I met Michael at a film club and he asked me for dinner at his house a few times, where I met Eileen.

I am an Italian and have a scholarship here in Leeds.

Michael gave me your address. He said I should come to see you if I came back to Italy in the summer.

I write to let you know that your brother has left his wife and departed for an unknown destination. His wife is not writing, first, because she knows almost no Italian and second, because she is very upset. Without judging Michael, I feel very sorry for her and I used to feel sorry for him, too, when I went to see him here in that filthy boardinghouse where he was holed up.

Eileen wants me to notify you of Michael's departure, first, because she doesn't know if he told you that their marriage had broken up, second, because Michael left no address, third, because he left various debts. She does not intend to pay these debts and asks that you pay them. Michael left debts of three hundred pounds. Eileen asks that you send her three hundred pounds and immediately if possible.

Ermanno Giustiniani
Lincoln Road 4, Leeds

34

May 3, 1971

Dear Ermanno Giustiniani,

Tell Eileen that I shall send her the money through a relative, Lillino Borghi, who is going to England shortly.

If in the meantime you have learned Michael's whereabouts, I would be grateful if you would let me know immediately. We have had no further news. He wrote me that he might go to Bruges, but I don't know whether he went there or elsewhere.

He had written that he had no friends in Leeds, but maybe that was before meeting you in that film club. Or maybe he lied about that and other things. Between his reticence and his possible lies I have a hard time figuring out his life. Certainly I don't pass judgment on him and besides I don't know any of the facts necessary to judge him. I can regret his lies and his silence, but there are circumstances that force us to lie or be silent against our wills.

131

I am not writing to Eileen directly because I know very little English and also I don't know what I could say to her other than that I'm grieved over what has happened to her. Maybe you can tell her this.

Angelica Vivanti De Righi

35

Trapani, May 15, 1971

Dear Michael,
Guess what. I am writing from a city in Sicily. I have ended up in Trapani. I don't know if I told you that in a boarding-house on Annibaliano Square, the boardinghouse was called Piave, anyway I made friends there with a woman who was very nice to me. Once she said she could give me and the baby a place to stay in Trapani. Then I completely lost track of her and I couldn't remember her last name, only her first name, which is Lillia. She is fat and has curly hair. From Novi Ligure I wrote to a maid at the Piave. I knew only her first name, which is Vincenza. I described the fat curly-haired woman with the little baby. The maid sent me the address in Trapani, where Curly Hair's husband has opened a snack bar. I wrote to her but didn't wait for an answer before leaving. So here I am. Her husband wasn't happy at all to see me but Curly Hair said that I would help her with the housework. I get up at seven in the morning and take coffee to Curly Hair, who stays in bed

wearing a bed jacket. Then I have to take care of the babies, mine and hers, go out and do the marketing, clean the house, and make the beds. For lunch Curly Hair gets something from the snack bar, usually lasagne, because she is very fond of lasagne. However, I don't think those lasagne or for that matter any of the dishes from the snack bar are very good. Curly Hair is unhappy in this city. She thinks it is dreary. In addition, the snack bar is not doing well at all. They have bank loans due. I offered to do the bookkeeping but her husband said I wasn't the type for that job and I guess he is right. Curly Hair often cries on my shoulder. I can't cheer her up because I am not very cheerful myself. However, the baby is well. In the afternoon I take him to the park with the other baby. Curly Hair has a baby carriage and they both fit into it. In the park I talk with everyone I meet and I tell lies. It is good to be with strangers when you are depressed. At least you can tell lies.

Curly Hair is certainly no stranger any more. I know every feature of her face. I know all her clothes, underwear, the rollers she uses to curl her hair. Every day I see her eating lasagne with her mouth smeared with tomato. I am no longer a stranger to her either. Sometimes she is rude to me and I give it right back to her. I don't tell her lies any more because there were times when I told her the truth and cried on her shoulder. I told her I have no one and that everyone has kicked me around.

Curly Hair's seven-month-old baby weighs 21 pounds; mine weighs only 14 pounds, but a pediatrician in Novi Ligure told me that babies don't have to be so fat. Besides, my baby is prettier and pinker and I must tell you that now he has curly blond hair, not really reddish like yours but reddish-blond and his eyes are not exactly green but a sort of gray-green. Sometimes, when he laughs, I think he looks like you but when he is asleep he doesn't look like you at all; he looks like my grandfather Gustav. Curly Hair says a blood test could prove whether or not he is your child, but that is not a sure thing. There aren't any sure ways to find out whose child one is. And in the end who cares. It doesn't matter to you and very little to me. Those twelve coveralls that your wife sent are very useful, I must admit. At first I hated them but now they are practical, and sometimes I put one on Curly Hair's baby, too, when I have nothing else.

In fact, I am a servant here. I don't like being a servant and I guess nobody likes it. At night I go to bed dead tired and my feet hurt. My room is behind the kitchen. The heat is killing. They don't treat me like a servant exactly and they don't pay me because they say I am sort of part of the family so they give me some five thousand lire now and then when they remember. Since I arrived, they have remembered only twice. Of course, they are having a hard time.

I have put my fur coat in a plastic bag and hung it in Curly Hair's closet. Every now and then Curly Hair unzips the bag and caresses a sleeve. She says she would like to buy it from me but I don't want to sell it to her because I am afraid she would pay me little or even nothing for it. Originally I planned not to sell it. I wanted to keep it as a souvenir of the time when I lived with the pelican but I will sell it because I am not sentimental. I have my sentimental moments, but they pass quickly and when I come to my senses, I get myself together and am cool and down to earth. However, Oswald says I am nearly always on some sort of emotional high and maybe that's true because I have had some real bad trips. I saw Oswald in the middle of April when I stopped in Rome on my way here. I went to the shop and there was Mrs. Schlitz who was very warm and friendly to me and the baby, and then Oswald came. I asked if he had news of you but he didn't. He had just returned from a trip in Umbria with Ada, of course. He drove me to the station. He told me that the pelican has gone to live in his house in Chianti and probably will close down the publishing firm because it doesn't interest him any more. Ada goes to see him in Chianti sometimes. The pelican means nothing to me any more, and the times when I was so broken up over him seem very far away. The important thing is to keep moving and to get away from things that cause pain. Oswald said that I wouldn't like it in Trapani and that they would make a servant of me, which is exactly what happened. I told him I would gradually find some other arrangement, maybe a job along the lines of the one I had in the publishing firm before the pelican lured me into his attic. Of course, he really didn't lure me; I forced myself in there. Anyway, Oswald had no suggestions, only that I shouldn't go to Trapani. What a big help. I knew perfectly well that I would die of boredom here in the evenings, but it's enough to avoid looking out the window and to get into bed and pull the covers over one's head.

Oswald waited on board the train until it left. He bought me magazines and sandwiches. He gave me money. I gave him my address in Trapani in case he decided to come and visit me. Then we embraced and kissed and while I was kissing him I realized he is a complete fag. I had doubts before but they all disappeared in that moment on the train.

My address is at the end of this letter. I don't know if I will stay here very long, because from time to time Curly Hair says she can't afford to keep me. Sometimes she talks this way, other times she puts her arms around me and says she likes and needs my company. I feel sorry for Curly Hair. At the same time I hate her. I have discovered that knowing people even slightly makes one feel sorry for them. I prefer to be with strangers because I don't yet pity and hate them.

I imagine the heat will be killing here in August. I am in my room as I write you. It has one window but in order to open it I have to stand on the bed. The weather is hot already. The snack bar is on the floor below and the very thought of it makes me feel even hotter. I am sitting on the bed writing to you and nearby I have a pile of stuff to iron. I am not going to iron them now, no way.

I am writing to your regular address in Leeds. Lots of times I wonder what sort of life you lead with your wife in that English city. Your life must be better than mine. Here there aren't any men who appeal to me. Sometimes I wonder where all the men who appeal to me and to whom I appeal are hiding.

Best for now.

Mara
Via Garibaldi 14, Trapani

36

Dear Mara,

I am writing you some very painful news. My brother Michael died in a student demonstration in Bruges. The police came and broke up the demonstration. He was followed by a group of Fascists, and one of them knifed him. It seems that they knew him. The street was empty. With Michael was a friend who went to call the Red Cross. Meanwhile, Michael lay alone on the sidewalk. The street was lined with warehouses, which were all closed at that hour, namely ten at night. Michael died at eleven o'clock in the hospital emergency room. His friend telephoned my sister Angelica who went to Bruges with her husband and Oswald Ventura. They brought Michael back to Italy and he was buried yesterday in Rome next to our father who, you may recall, died last December.

Oswald asked me to write you. He is too upset. As you can imagine, I am upset also but I am trying to be strong.

The news appeared in all the newspapers, but Oswald said that you don't read the papers.

I know you were fond of my brother and that you wrote to each other. You and I met at a birthday party for Michael last year. I remember you very well. We felt we ought to let you know of our great loss.

Viola

37

June 12, 1971

Dear Mara,

I know Viola has written you. I am staying at my mother's house with my little girl. I keep my mother company and together we live through the days of paralysis that follow a tragedy, days of paralysis even though we fill them with things to do, letters to be written, photographs to be looked at, and days of silence even though we force ourselves to talk as much as possible, and to keep busy with the living. At times we live on memories, preferably those that seem most innocuous because they are the most remote; at other times we steep ourselves in the minutiae of the present. We talk and laugh out loud to reassure ourselves that we can still think of the present and haven't lost our voices. But the minute we are quiet we hear our silence. Oswald comes every now and then. His presence affects neither our silence nor our paralysis and so his visits are welcome.

I would like to know if Michael had written you any letters in the days before he died. He did not write to us.

Those who killed him are still at large and the recollections of the boy who saw them are confused and vague. I think that Michael got involved with political groups, this time in Bruges, and that those who killed him did so for specific reasons. But this is only guesswork on my part. Actually, we know nothing, and all we may be able to discover will lead to more guesses that we will then continue to question in our minds without ever finding a clear answer.

I can't bear to think of certain things, especially of those moments when Michael lay alone in that street. I can't bear to think that while he was dying, I was quietly at home, washing dishes, washing Flora's socks, hanging them out on the balcony with two clothespins and going through the evening routine until the moment when the phone rang. I cannot bear to think of what I did the day before because everything proceeded peacefully up to the ring of that telephone. Michael gave my telephone number to the boy who was with him in the brief time he regained consciousness. He died immediately after, and I am haunted by the thought that he remembered my telephone number as he was dying. I understood nothing on the phone because I don't know any German so I called Oreste who speaks German. Afterward, Oreste coped with everything, taking our little girl to our friends, the Bettoias, calling Oswald, calling Viola, who went to tell our mother. I wanted to be the one to tell her but I was anxious to leave for Bruges and in the end I decided to leave because I wanted to say good-bye to Michael and to see his curly red hair one last time.

We saw Michael in the chapel of the hospital. Then we fetched his suitcase, his loden coat, and red sweater from the boardinghouse. They were on a chair in his room. He was wearing jeans and a white T-shirt with a tiger's head on it when he died. We saw the jeans and the shirt stained with blood at the police station. In his suitcase we found some underwear, a package of crumbled crackers, and a train schedule. We went to see the street where they killed him. It was a narrow street bordered by storage depots for cement. At that time of day it was full of noise and trucks. Michael's friend, the one who was with him when he died, came with us. He is a seventeen-year-old Dane. He showed us the beer hall where he had eaten lunch with Michael and then the movie theater where they had gone that afternoon. They had known each other for three days. We were unable to find out anything from him about Michael's other friends or the people with whom he was in contact. And so the only things we know about his days in that city are the boardinghouse, the beer hall, and the movie theater.

Send me news of yourself and your baby. I think of your baby from time to time now because Michael told me it might be his. When I saw the baby, I didn't think he looked like Michael, but he could be Michael's child. I think we, that is, my mother, my sister, and I should try to help your baby regardless of whether or not he is Michael's. I don't really know the reason why I feel we ought to do this, but then not everything we ought to do can be explained. In fact, I think our duties are inexplicable. So we shall try to send you some money from time to time, not that money solves your problems, since you are an aimless drifter, a lonely foolish girl. However, the thought of wandering aimlessly and in total solitude has a great appeal, since there is something of the drifter and the fool in all of us and to that extent we can put ourselves in your place and understand you.

Angelica

38

Trapani, June 18, 1971

Dear Mrs. Angelica,

I am a friend of Mara's and I am writing to you because Mara is too upset to write. Mara asks that I express to you her grief over the great misfortune you have suffered, and I join her in sending my most sincere condolences. Mara is so upset by this tragedy that she hasn't eaten for two days. It is understandable, given the fact that your late brother Michael was the father of that little angel Paul Michael, an adorable creature who at this very moment is playing on the balcony with my own dear baby. In the name of these two little innocents I pray that you not forget Mara who is staying with me at the present time to help me with the housework. I do not think I can keep her and her angelic baby much longer because it is a financial burden and while I feel for Mara as if she were my sister I really need some help with the housework and Mara has too many worries for her to do the work which requires patience, care, and willingness. However, neither I nor my husband has the heart to put her out on the street. I ask therefore that all of you assume the responsibility for this young girl prematurely bereft and the innocent little orphan of your son prematurely flown to heaven. I have lots of worries and troubles and endless money problems. I have done my part but I don't want to deprive others of their chance to do both their duty and at the same time a generous act.

With kindest regards and assuring you of my respectful best wishes and trusting that my appeal will not go unheard.

Lillia Savio Lavia

P.S. I call to your attention that in having Mara with you you will have the great consolation of seeing the features of your beloved dead in the little angel and this consolation will come like a healing dew to hearts prostrate with grief, which cannot be comforted.

39

Dear Angelica,

I am here in Varese staying with an uncle of Oswald's. As Oswald will have told you, Curly Hair and her husband kicked me out. Thanks a lot for the money you sent. Unfortunately, I had to give most of it to Curly Hair. She claimed I broke an entire service of china, which I did. One day, when she had a dozen or so relatives for dinner, I bumped the tray against the door and all the dishes fell and smashed on the floor.

When I learned that Michael was dead, I threw myself on the bed and cried for the whole day. Curly Hair kept bringing me soup. She really wasn't mean when she quit thinking about housework and money. Then I pulled myself together out of love for my baby and went on living my usual life and Curly Hair gave me vitamin shots because I was run down.

I didn't let Curly Hair read your letter and I kept all my letters hidden in a pair of boots. One day I went into my room and there was Curly Hair standing in front of the bureau. She blushed and said she was looking for the lemon squeezer. I replied that I knew perfectly well that she was there because she wanted to rummage through my things and then we had a fight, a real fight and for the first time yelled and screamed and I tore a flounce on her bathrobe. Then on the day your money order came we had another fight, yelling and screaming, and I realized it was pointless to go on that way. I cashed the money order and threw the money in her face. She took the money. This happened a few days before I left. I realize that all my life my relationships with people sour after a while. Maybe it is my fault, maybe theirs. I don't know. Anyway my relationship with Curly Hair fell apart. I realize that I should be grateful to her but now I can't think of her calmly or affectionately.

It was very good of you to send me that money and please thank your mother as well, because I imagine that she gave you the money. When you want to send me money, I will thank you and accept it but I must tell you something in all honesty. I don't think my baby is Michael's. He doesn't look like him. Sometimes he looks like my grandfather Gustav. Other times he looks like Oliviero, that boy who was often with Michael and who always wore a gray sweater with two forest green stripes. I don't know if you remember Oliviero. I slept with him three or four times, and didn't like him, but maybe it just could have happened with him. In your letter you put it so nicely about how I am foolish and a drifter and that nevertheless you can understand. Even if I am a fool and a drifter, I wanted to tell you the truth because I don't want to cheat you. I may be inclined to cheat everyone else but I really don't want to cheat you. As you say, one cannot explain why one feels one must or must not act in a certain way. I think it is a good thing that it can't be explained because if everything could be explained one would die of boredom.

Now I will tell you about the disaster. Curly Hair and her

husband took a trip to Catania. They were supposed to be away for three days but the car broke down. So they came back early and when they came into the house they found me in their double bed with their brother-in-law. It was Sunday at three in the afternoon.

This brother-in-law was really his brother and her brother-in-law. He was eighteen. I say "was" because I won't see him any more. He was at the dinner when I dropped all the dishes and he helped me pick up the pieces. Anyway, that Sunday I was alone in the house since they had gone to Catania, as I said. I was putting the babies to bed, mine and theirs, for their afternoon nap. It was terribly hot. Peppino had the keys to the house and suddenly there he was. I hadn't heard the door open and I was frightened. He was tall with thick black hair. He had been dogging my footsteps ever since that day of the smashed dishes. He looked a little like Oliviero. I closed the blinds in the children's room and we went into the kitchen. He said he was hungry and wanted me to make him something to eat but I didn't feel like cooking so I gave him a plate of lasagne. He said he hated those cold lasagne from the snack bar and that he knew how they were cooked, namely with the same old oil used over and over and kept in a bowl and how the sauce was made from the meat left on the plates of patrons. So we began to chat, criticizing the snack bar and therefore also Curly Hair and her husband, his sister-in-law and brother, and by way of talking we ended up in their bed because my bed was too small. I showed him my bed but he said theirs was much better. We had finished making love only a short while and were lying peacefully in each other's arms half asleep in the darkened room when all of a sudden I saw Curly Hair's head and then her husband's bald head and dark glasses in the doorway. Peppino immediately jumped into his pants and pulled on his undershirt and shirt and I guess he must have finished dressing on his way down the stairs because he got out very fast, leaving me with those two vipers. They told me to get out immediately and I said I wanted to wait until the baby finished his nap. Meanwhile both babies were awake and crying. I went to pack my suitcase and Curly Hair came and suddenly began to cry, saying she understood me but her husband refused to understand and he felt I had defiled their bed with his brother and corrupted their home and the innocence of the babies. Curly Hair prepared the baby's milk for me in a plastic bottle. I asked her for a thermos, but she wouldn't give it to me because she had only one and she had already given one to me at the boardinghouse, which I had lost somewhere along the line. The bottle may not have been clean because the milk went bad and I had to throw it out that evening. I told her I was leaving and going to Rome, but I didn't leave and went instead to a woman whom I knew who ran a bakery. The shop was closed but I rang the back doorbell. She said I could sleep there one night but no more and she fixed a cot for me under the stairs. I put the baby in his plastic carrier but it is hot for him to sleep in that. At Curly Hair's he slept in an old crib. That night I caught up with Peppino by telephoning him at the snack bar and he came and we went out walking and then we made love in a field near the railroad tracks. While we were making love, I was thinking I don't give a damn about Peppino. I never feel involved with boys younger than me. I can only fall in love with older men who seem to have strange secrets and depressions—like the pelican. But I have great fun with the younger ones and I feel very gay and at the same time I feel sorry for them because they seem stupid and silly like me and I begin to feel as if I were by myself, only much happier. That is the way it was with Michael. I had a lot of fun with him and we had some marvelous times together, which had nothing to do with real love. They were like the hours I spent as a child playing tag with other children on the street. All of a sudden, as I lay there with Peppino, I began to think of Michael and to cry. Then I knew that I can't ever be happy for very long and I will never succeed in being happy for any length of time because I remember and think about too many things. Peppino thought I was crying because Curly Hair had kicked me out and he tried to console me as best he could by mewing like a cat. He could do a perfect imitation of a cat mewing, but I continued to sob, thinking of Michael who died murdered on the street and thinking that maybe I will end up dead some night killed on some street corner, who knows where, and far from my baby. Then I began to think about my baby whom I had left with the woman in the bakery. So I told Peppino to quit mewing because it didn't amuse me and then suddenly I remembered that in my hurry to leave Curly Hair's I had forgotten my fur coat, which was still there in the clothes-bag in her closet. So the next day Peppino went in with his key and got it and brought it to me at the bakery. Actually, he didn't want to go because he was afraid of meeting them on the stairs, but I begged him so much that he finally agreed and he didn't run into them. I sold the coat to a friend of the bakery woman for four hundred thousand lire and went to a motel. From there I telephoned Oswald at his shop in Rome. He said he would think about where I could go and then he called back to say that I could stay with an uncle of his in Varese, an old gentleman who was looking for someone to sleep in the house so he would not be alone at night. So here I am in a lovely house with a garden full of hydrangeas. I am bored but otherwise all right; the baby is well. Oswald's uncle is quite nice, maybe queer. He is elegant and smells of cologne and wears beautiful black velvet jackets. He doesn't work. At one time he dealt in paintings and the house is full of them. Above all, he is deaf as a post so he doesn't hear the baby cry at night. I have a pretty room with flowered wallpaper. No comparison with that hole where I slept in Trapani and best of all I hardly have to do anything except cut the hydrangeas and put them in vases and in the evening make two poached eggs, one for Oswald's uncle and one for myself. The only trouble is that I don't know how long I can stay here because the uncle says that Ada may send him her butler, and if Ada does this he won't need me. Ada always gets in my way. She should drop dead. I would stay here forever. I think I can put up with the boredom. The only thing is that sometimes I am afraid in this lonely house. I never used to be afraid, but now at a certain point a sort of terror grabs me and I feel my throat tighten. I remember Michael and I begin to think that I, too, will die and maybe I will die right here in this pretty house with the red carpet on the stairs and the decorated fixtures in the bathrooms and vases of hydrangeas even in the kitchen and the doves cooing on the window sills.

Mara

40

Dear Philip,

Yesterday I saw you in the Spanish Square. I don't think you saw me. I was with Angelica and Flora. You were alone. Angelica thought you had aged. I don't know what I thought. You were wearing your jacket on your shoulders and made your usual gesture of rubbing your brow while you walked. You went into Babington's.

I found it extremely odd to see you pass by and not to call you, but we wouldn't really have anything in particular to say to each other. I don't much care about what is going on in your life and certainly you don't care about mine. I don't care because I am unhappy. You don't care because you are happy. Anyway, today you and I are strangers.

I know you came to the cemetery. I was not at the cemetery. Viola told me you were there. I know you told her you wanted to come and see me. Up to now you haven't come. I don't want to see you. Generally, I don't want to see anyone except my daughters with their inescapable family complications, my sister-in-law Matilde and our friend Oswald Ventura. While I am not conscious of wanting these people's company, I miss them if I don't see them for several days. Maybe if you came to see me, I would immediately get used to you and I don't want to accustom myself to the presence of someone who, given the circumstances, cannot be counted on. That pink little creature you married would never allow you to come often.

Because you may have become utterly stupid in the time since we used to see each other, I hasten to explain that there is no bitterness of any kind in the words "pink little creature." Whatever jealousy or bitterness I might have felt toward you has been purged by everything that has happened to me.

Every so often I think of you. This morning I suddenly remembered the day when you and I went in your car to visit Michael, who was in camp at Courmayeur. Michael must have been about twelve at the time. I remember seeing him standing in front of his tent, nude to the waist and wearing climbing boots. I was delighted to see him looking so healthy, tanned, covered with freckles. Sometimes in town he looked so pale. He rarely went out doors. His father never told him to go out. We drove around in the mountains and then stopped at an inn for tea. As a rule, Michael made you nervous. You didn't like him and he didn't like you. You said he was a spoiled, willful, conceited brat. He thought that you were disagreeable. He didn't say so but clearly he thought so. However, that day everything went well and peacefully without any harsh words between you. We went into a shop where they sold postcards and souvenirs. You bought him a green hat with a chamois tail. He was delighted and wore it tilted on top of his curly hair. He may have been spoiled but he could also be amused with next to nothing. In the car he began to sing a song his father always sang. Usually that annoyed me because it reminded me of his father, about whom I felt very bitter at that time. But I was content that day and all my bitterness grew light and sweet. The song went, *"Non avemo ni canones—ni tanks ni aviones—oi Carmelà."* And you knew the song and continued, *"El terror de los fascistas—rumba —larumba—larumba—là."* You will think it stupid, but I have written this letter to thank you for having sung with Michael that day and also for having bought him the hat with the chamois tail, which he wore for two or three years. I would like to ask you as a favor to send me the words of that song by mail if you know them. You may think it strange, but one has very minimal and odd wishes when in fact one desires nothing.

Adriana

41

Ada had left for London with Elisabeth. Oswald was to fetch them at the beginning of September. Now he was still busy in his shop. It was the twentieth of August. Angelica was about to leave on a motor trip with Oreste, their little girl, and the Bettoias. Viola was staying with Adriana. The twins were at camp in the Dolomites.

Angelica and Viola had taken Ada and Elisabeth to the airport in Viola's car. Now they were returning to the city and Oswald followed them in his car.

That morning Angelica and Viola had gone with Lillino to a notary and signed the papers for the sale of the tower. The pelican had bought the tower. He did not come to the notary's but sent his lawyer. He continued to stay in Chianti and, according to Oswald, suffered from various ailments that although imaginary were no less painful. He never left his house in Chianti. Ada ran his publishing firm. She didn't get paid but then Ada didn't care about money, Angelica told Viola. She was sitting next to Viola, who was driving. Angelica examined her delicate profile, her long lustrous hair that had been brushed back in long strokes and stayed neatly in place in spite of the intense heat, the freshness of her white linen dress. Angelica was wearing jeans and a wrinkled shirt. She had spent the afternoon packing for her departure the next day.

Ada didn't care about money, Angelica said, and anyway she had plenty. The pelican didn't care about money and he had a great deal of it. It was hard to see why he had bought the tower. He certainly would never set foot in it. He had not even seen it. Ada must have convinced him that it would be a good investment. Ada planned to remodel the tower into a restaurant or maybe a rest home. "A fine rest," Viola said. It was exhausting to climb to the tower.

"You haven't seen it. I have," Viola said.

"But I am telling you Ada will remodel it completely," Angelica said. "She will have a road put in and a pool and cottages and who knows what all."

According to Angelica, Ada and the pelican shared a common curiosity about money and the way things could be changed by means of money. They both were equally indifferent about having money and spending it, since they had so much. The difference between them lay in the fact that Ada could not think of herself as being without money while the pelican spent his entire life imagining himself as poor and feeling chills and tremors of horror and excitement up and down his spine.

"So that takes care of our tower," Viola said.

"It never was ours," Angelica said.

"It wasn't a nice place, really," Viola said.

"I am sure it wasn't."

"From the outside it was a pile of stones with a window at the top. It was shaped vaguely like a tower, but in that case any old pile of rocks can be called a tower. Inside it smelled of manure and in fact there was a lot of manure scattered about. That's what I remember mostly, the manure."

"But he doesn't smell odors," Angelica said

"Who?"

"The pelican. He has that nose but says he smells nothing."

"Anyway it's impossible to understand why he or our father bought it."

"If Ada said it was a good investment, Ada is sure to be right."

"Then it makes no sense for us to have sold it," Viola said.

"Lillino said to."

"And what if he gave us bad advice?"

"Well, it's done."

"I couldn't figure out what to do with that tower of manure," Viola said. "Still, our father had bought it and I am sorry I called it a 'tower of manure.' I said it without thinking. Anyway we have sold it and as far as we are concerned the matter is finished."

"Assuming it was ever begun," Angelica said.

"I feel miserable at the thought of being alone with Mother in that lonely house," Viola said. "I don't like lonely places. That was another reason why I didn't like the tower."

"There is Matilde," Angelica said.

"She doesn't make me feel one bit less miserable."

"There is the telephone. You seem to have forgotten that now there is a phone in the house. Installed a week ago, thanks to Ada. And there will be Ada's dog. Oswald is going to bring it."

"I can't bear dogs," Viola said. "I am going to have to look after the dog, the rabbits, and the twins' lamb which has to be fed milk with a baby's bottle. They could at least have taken the lamb with them."

"To the Dolomites?"

"I'm afraid I'm pregnant," Viola said. "I'm terribly late."

"That's fine. You always say you want a baby."

"I'm afraid because I will be in that isolated house without a doctor nearby."

"You can telephone Dr. Bovo. He will come right away. Anyway, it can't be helped. We can't leave mother alone there. Matilde sleeps like a log. Not even an earthquake would wake her up. Cloti is on vacation. I have to leave for a few days because I promised Flora. I will be back soon and then you can leave."

"I know. I'm not arguing. I simply want to say I feel miserable and if I want to say so I don't know why I shouldn't. Elio left for Holland yesterday. He was terribly upset about going without me."

"He could have stayed with you."

"It wasn't so much that he wanted to go to Holland but he needed a change. Poor Elio. Michael's death upset him terribly. He blames himself for not going to Leeds when Michael got married. He says he could have given him some useful advice."

"What sort of advice?"

"I don't know. Advice. Elio is a very understanding person."

"Michael was murdered. I wonder what sort of understanding and advice could have protected him from the Fascists who murdered him."

"If he had stayed quietly in Leeds they wouldn't have killed him."

"Maybe he found it hard to be quiet."

"The last time I saw him, he was coming out of that rotisserie in Largo Argentina. He said, 'Hi' and walked away immediately. I asked him what he had bought. He said, 'A roast chicken.' Those are the last words he said to me. What sad words. I watched him as he left with his paper bag. A stranger."

They arrived at their mother's house. Viola parked the

car near the two miniature fir trees, which looked limp and exhausted from the heat. Angelica took the suitcases down from the luggage rack.

"You have certainly brought a lot of stuff with you," she said.

" 'A roast chicken,' " Viola said. "His last words. I can still hear him saying them. And to think we were so close to each other as children. We played at mother and daughter with dolls. I was the mother, he the daughter. He wanted to be a little girl. He wanted to be like me. But later on he changed. He despised me. He said I was middle-class, but I don't know how to be otherwise. Later on you were the only one he liked. I was very jealous of you. Certainly you must remember many things about him. You saw lots of him, were a friend of his friends. I only knew their names. Gianni, Anselmo, Oliviero, Oswald. As to Oswald, I was always very much against their friendship. It was a homosexual friendship and there is no getting away from that. It was enough to see them together. Elio said so and he had seen them together. I still can't accept the fact that Michael became a homosexual. He would say that I am square. It bothers me to see Oswald. He is nice, perfectly pleasant, but it upsets me to meet him. I'll see him often because he comes here often. Who knows why he comes. There he is now. I recognize the sound of his car. Still, Mother likes him. Either she doesn't think about it or she knows and is used to it. I guess one gets used to anything."

"One gets used to anything when there is nothing left," Angelica said.

42

Dear Angelica,

I arrived in Leeds yesterday morning. I spent the night at a boardinghouse called The Hong-Kong. You can't imagine anything more depressing than The Hong-Kong in Leeds.

I left Ada and Elisabeth in London, since there was no point in their coming here.

I was able to locate that young man Ermanno Giustiniana who had written to you. He is still here at the address you gave me. He is a nice boy with a pale pointed face and a Malaysian cast to his features. In fact he said his mother was an Asiatic.

He said that Eileen and the children have gone back to America. He doesn't know the address. According to him Eileen was a woman of great intelligence but she was an alcoholic. Michael married her with a view to reforming her. It sounds like him because he liked to be called upon to help others. However, his generosity was useless because it was too brief. The marriage broke up after eight days.

They seemed happy for eight days. Ermanno didn't know them during those days. He met them afterward, when it was all more or less over, but mutual acquaintances told him that during those eight days Eileen had stopped drinking and was another person.

Ermanno took me to the house on Nelson Road where Eileen and Michael had lived. There was a "For Sale" sign on it, so I went to the real estate agent and was able to see the inside. It is a small English house, one room to a floor, and furnished with awful fake modern furniture. I went in all the rooms. In the kitchen I saw an apron with pictures of carrots and tomatoes on it and a black raincoat with a torn sleeve, which I guess were probably Eileen's. In another room there were pictures of Snow White and the Seven Dwarfs on the walls and a bowl of sour milk on the floor, apparently left by a cat. I am describing all this in detail because I think you would like to know it. I found nothing of Michael's except for a woolen undershirt that had been used as a dust cloth and was hanging on the handle of a broom. I thought I recognized it as an undershirt he had bought for the winter and in fact I found that it still had the label from that shop Anticoli in Via della Vite. After a moment of indecision I left it there. I don't think there is any point in keeping things that belonged to the dead when these things have been used by strangers and lost their identity.

The visit to that house has plunged me into a deep depression. I am writing to you from my room in the boardinghouse and from the window I can see Leeds, one of the last cities Michael knew. I can't get much out of Ermanno Giustiniana about Michael, either because he hardly knew him or barely remembers him or maybe because it saddens him to talk about Michael at any length with me. I will dine with him this evening. He is a nice boy but still a boy. Young people today don't remember anything. They have no sense of the past and above all they make no effort to remember. As you well know, Michael had no memory, or, rather, he never tried to retain and cherish the past. We are the only people who try to remember, you, your mother, and I; you by natural disposition and your mother and I by inclination and also because there is nothing in our lives at present that can compare with the moments and places we experienced in the course of our lives. While I was living these experiences, they had an extraordinary intensity because I knew that later I would turn to recall them. I was always much saddened by the fact that Michael never wanted or was unable to experience this intensity and that he went forward without ever so much as a backward glance. However, I think that he felt this intensity in me without realizing it. And many times I have thought that maybe while he was dying he suddenly discovered the past and looked back. I find this a consoling thought. One comforts oneself with nothing when there is nothing else. Even the sight of that ragged shirt that I left in the kitchen gave me a strange sad and icy consolation.

Oswald